POINT GUARD

ALSO BY MIKE LUPICA

The Only Game

The Extra Yard

A
HOME TEAM
NOVEL

POINT GUARD

MIKE LUPICA

SIMON & SCHUSTER BOOKS FOR YOUNG READERS
NEW YORK LONDON TORONTO SYDNEY NEW DELHI

SIMON & SCHUSTER BOOKS FOR YOUNG READERS
An imprint of Simon & Schuster Children's Publishing Division
1230 Avenue of the Americas, New York, New York 10020
This book is a work of fiction. Any references to historical events, real people,
or real places are used fictitiously. Other names, characters, places, and events are
products of the author's imagination, and any resemblance to actual events or
places or persons, living or dead, is entirely coincidental.
Text copyright © 2017 by Mike Lupica
Jacket illustration copyright © 2017 by Dave Seeley
All rights reserved, including the right of reproduction
in whole or in part in any form.
SIMON & SCHUSTER BOOKS FOR YOUNG READERS
is a trademark of Simon & Schuster, Inc.
For information about special discounts for bulk purchases, please contact Simon
& Schuster Special Sales at 1-866-506-1949 or business@simonandschuster.com.
The Simon & Schuster Speakers Bureau can bring authors to your live event. For
more information or to book an event, contact the Simon & Schuster Speakers
Bureau at 1-866-248-3049 or visit our website at www.simonspeakers.com.
Book design by Lucy Ruth Cummins
The text for this book was set in Adobe Garamond Pro.
Manufactured in the United States of America
0217 FFG
First Edition
2 4 6 8 10 9 7 5 3 1
Library of Congress Cataloging-in-Publication Data
Names: Lupica, Mike, author.
Title: Point guard / Mike Lupica.
Description: First edition. | New York : Simon & Schuster Books for Young
Readers, [2017] | Series: The home team | Summary: "It's basketball season for the
home team but Gus must wrestle with prejudice when he's the only one bothered
by Cassie joining the boys' team and his teammate Steve makes
fun of Gus's Dominican heritage"—Provided by publisher.
Identifiers: LCCN 2016013148 (print) | LCCN 2016039828 (eBook) (print) |
LCCN 2016039828 (eBook) | ISBN 9781481410038 (hardback) |
ISBN 978-1-4814-1006-9 (eBook) | ISBN 9781481410069 (eBook)
Subjects: | CYAC: Basketball—Fiction. | Friendship—Fiction. | Prejudices—
Fiction. | Dominican Americans—Fiction. | BISAC: JUVENILE FICTION /
Sports & Recreation / General. | JUVENILE FICTION / Social Issues /
Friendship. | JUVENILE FICTION / Social Issues
/ General (see also headings under Family).
Classification: LCC PZ7.L97914 Po 2017 (print) | LCC PZ7.L97914 (eBook) |
DDC [Fic]—dc23
LC record available at https://lccn.loc.gov/2016013148

This book is for my mom, Lee Lupica,
who keeps reminding us how big her heart is

ONE

This was how it happened sometimes:

You didn't want to stop, no matter how long you'd been playing.

That was the way Gus Morales felt right now in the gym at Walton Middle School, playing one last game of two-on-two with his best friends in the world.

It was Gus and Teddy Madden against Jack Callahan and Cassie Bennett. Jack and Cassie had won the first game. Gus and Teddy had won the second. Now the score was 10–10 in the third, game to eleven baskets, you had to win by two.

Gus had been feeling it from the start, making left-handed shots from all over the court even with Jack guarding him most of the time. And Jack Callahan could guard anybody, because Jack was one of those guys who took as much pride in his defense as he did in his offense.

But Jack wasn't the problem right now.

Cassie was.

She was suddenly matching Gus shot for shot, as if they were playing a game of H-O-R-S-E. Jack had carried their offense for much of the first two games, but not only had Cassie gotten hot, Teddy was getting tired chasing her. It was a bad combination for Gus and Teddy's team. No, check that. It was a *terrible* combination. And Jack was taking great pleasure in feeding Cassie the ball. He knew Gus Morales as well as anybody, and he knew that as much as Gus hated losing, he really hated losing to Cassie. In anything.

It was just pickup basketball, friends going against friends. It wasn't the league championship football game Gus and Teddy and the Walton Wildcats had lost the previous Saturday to the Norris Panthers. Jack hadn't been out there with them because he'd hurt his shoulder early in the season and hadn't been cleared to play sports again until today.

But this two-on-two game still felt like a championship after the way they'd been going at each other for an hour. Maybe it was just the championship of this one afternoon, and having the gym to themselves, which always made them feel like they'd won some kind of lottery. Maybe this was just one more occasion when they were playing for the championship of each other.

Everybody on the court wanted to win.

More importantly? Nobody wanted to lose.

Jack had just gotten a put-back after a rare Cassie miss to tie the game. They were playing winners out, which meant they kept the ball if they scored. Jack had it on the left side. Gus backed off, practically daring him to shoot. Usually that was a huge mistake, because when the games counted, you always wanted the ball in Jack Callahan's hands. But Gus could see that Jack was having too much fun being Cassie's assist man down the stretch to think about hoisting one up. It never changed, even as they went from sport to sport and season to season: the only stat that ever mattered to Jack was the final score.

Jack dribbled to his left now, stopped suddenly, then whipped a pass across the court to Cassie, who was to the right of the foul line.

"Teddy," she said as soon as she caught the ball, in a singsong voice, "I'm coming for you."

"Leave me alone," Teddy said, giving her some room, hands on his knees and looking officially gassed.

"That is a big old no-can-do," she said. "It's you and me, big boy."

Teddy kept his eyes on Cassie but found enough energy to yell over to Gus and Jack, "Make the bad girl stop."

He was done, though. They all knew it. He had been trying to keep up with Cassie for three close games, finding out for himself what anyone who'd ever tried to cover Cassie already knew: chasing her was like chasing the wind. She was as fast dribbling the ball as she was without it. And she could shoot. Boy, could this girl shoot.

She could also chirp, the way she had just now, telling Teddy she was coming for him, calling him out one last time today, maybe even about to call her shot.

Gus wasn't much of a trash-talker. Neither was Jack. Neither was Teddy, as funny as he was. But all of Cassie's talk was just part of who she was, and they accepted it, mostly because she could back it all up.

She started her dribble with her right hand and took a hard, quick first step, as if she was about to drive past Teddy. But as soon as he bit on the move and backed up even more, Cassie stepped back. She created some very nice space for herself, and put up another set shot that seemed to float all the way up to the rafters before it finally came down, softly, through the net.

It was 11–10 for her team.

Still their ball.

This time, though, Cassie rushed her shot, trying to end things right here, and missed. Teddy got the rebound, threw the ball out to Gus.

They had a chance to tie.

Maybe it was going to take another hour for somebody to get ahead by two baskets.

Fine by Gus.

Jack came running out and got right up on Gus before Gus started his dribble.

"Gonna be like that, huh?" Gus said.

"Would you want it any other way?"

They both knew the answer. All four of them on the court knew. You couldn't be in this group and not throw everything you had at the other guy.

Or girl.

Gus decided to try a move he'd been practicing in his driveway. He was going to put the ball down with his left hand, as if he was the one who wanted to drive that way. But as soon as he did, he was going to whirl and go to the right. Using his right hand, his off hand, was something else he'd been working on as he got ready for basketball tryouts this Saturday. Might as well show it off now to the best defender in Walton.

Gus tried to sell Jack on the idea that he was going left again. Jack moved with him, overplaying, trying to cut him off. As soon as he did, Gus planted his right foot, spun around so he was facing the basket at the other end, and put the ball on his right hand, ready to cut to the middle, feeling Jack on his hip, knowing he had a step on him, at least.

As he did, he heard Teddy yell, "Gus!"

Too late.

Cassie had made her move as Gus made his, doubling him from behind, stealing the ball cleanly, turning defense into offense that fast.

She dribbled back out to the top of the key because that was the rule; you had to take it back there after any change of possession. As she did, Teddy pointed to Gus, telling him to take her, as Teddy moved over to guard Jack.

"Been wishing you'd make this switch all day," Cassie said, smiling.

"Didn't you ever hear the one about being careful what you wish for?" Gus said.

Cassie didn't answer. She was looking into his eyes, still smiling. As much as Gus was enjoying the moment, Cassie was clearly enjoying it more. This was exactly where she wanted to be. This was Cassie, 100 percent.

She dribbled with her right hand, then with her left, then her right again, as if she had the ball on some kind of string. Gus told himself not to watch the ball, to watch *her*, try to get a read on whether she was going to drive or pull back the way she just had on Teddy.

She decided to pass instead, off her last dribble with her right hand, her eyes never leaving Gus's.

Gus took his eyes off Cassie, though, just for a split second. He wanted to see where Jack was, how open he was, decide in another split second if Teddy needed help.

As soon as he did, Cassie broke for the basket, and the ball came right back to her: a perfect give-and-go. Gus scrambled to catch up, but now he was chasing her in vain the way Teddy had, watching as Cassie took Jack's bounce pass in stride and made the layup that won the game for their team.

Cassie stood underneath the basket, hands on hips, staring at Gus and looking like the happiest kid in Walton.

Gus said, "Is this the one where you tell us that girls rule and boys drool?"

"Never," she said. "I find that sort of trash talk *sooooo* uninteresting."

"On what planet?" Gus said.

Cassie laughed. So did he. Even now, he didn't want the day to be over. But it was all right, he told himself. The basketball season was just starting.

Gus Morales just had no way of knowing it wasn't going to be the season he expected.

Not even close.

TWO

I've figured something out," Gus said.

They were finally done for the day. Cassie's mom was coming in fifteen minutes to pick up everybody except Teddy,
who could walk home from the gym.

"First time for everything," Cassie said.

"You don't know what I'm going to say."

"No, I meant you figuring out something."

She was grinning at him.

"Wait," she said. "I think I do know what it is. You figured out today that I'm the best athlete our age in Walton. Not only that, you're ready to admit that because of the way we just closed out you losers."

They were all seated on the bottom row of the bleachers. Jack was at the far end. They all knew, even Cassie, that Jack Callahan was the best athlete their age in Walton, boy or girl. But all three of the boys knew they were just opening themselves up to heartbreak by pointing that fact out to her.

"The only thing better than you, Cass, is having our own private gym," he said.

"Way to change the subject," Cassie said.

Now Teddy grinned. "When the subject is you, does it ever really change?"

"Ha-ha," Cassie said.

Teddy shrugged and said, "Hey, a laugh is a laugh."

Their gym teacher, Mr. Howser, had agreed to let them shoot around today after the four of them offered to put away all the folding chairs the eighth graders had used for their last-period assembly. Of course Cassie had demanded they play two-on-two. She had even picked the teams. And they all knew that if Gus and Teddy had won the rubber game, she would have wanted them to play another game of seven baskets. Or five. Or even three.

MIKE LUPICA

For Cassie Bennett, the last basket was the only way to have the last word.

"Shocker," Gus had said, "you wanting to be with Jack."

"Size against speed," Cassie had said.

"Yeah," Gus had said. "Go with that."

She was the best girl athlete in town, in their grade and maybe any grade. But that was as far as Gus would go. He was, after all, a guy.

Cassie sighed now. "Okay, what have you figured out?"

"That I like basketball even more than I like baseball," Gus said.

They all turned to stare at him.

"Now that right there," Teddy said, "is some crazy talk."

"Absolutely no way you mean that," Jack said.

"I do," Gus said. "Absolutely."

"You expect us to believe that you're a basketball guy and not a baseball guy?" Teddy said. "No way. Not buying it."

"I didn't say I wasn't a baseball guy," Gus said. "I just said I'm feeling like I'm more of a basketball guy now." He put out his hands. "Hey, I put a lot of thought into this."

Cassie nodded. "Had to happen eventually."

"The basketball thing?" Gus said.

She smiled, like she just couldn't help herself. Or was just amusing herself—again. "No," she said. "The thought thing."

"Funny," Gus said.

"I know," Cassie said.

"Gus," Jack said, "your dad told me one time that back in the Dominican when people talked about the American dream, they meant the dream of coming to America to play baseball in the big leagues."

They all knew Gus's family history: both of his parents had moved to New York City with their parents and had grown up in a section of the city—Washington Heights—that Gus told his friends had the most Dominicans this side of Santo Domingo, the capital and biggest city in the Dominican Republic.

"But even my dad is as happy watching basketball now as he is watching baseball, especially if LeBron or Steph Curry is playing," Gus said. "He says that basketball is the most American game now."

Teddy said, "But aren't you the guy who always told us that someday you were going to hit home runs in the big leagues the way David Ortiz did?"

David Ortiz was Dominican born, and had ended up hitting more than five hundred home runs and helping the Red Sox win three World Series. In 2004, when they'd won their first since 1918, the other hitting star on the team was Manny Ramirez, another Dominican American, and one who had grown up in Washington Heights.

Gus shrugged. "And maybe I'll still do that. But I'm just telling you guys that right now, I am more fired up for this basketball season than any season I've ever played."

"You sure that's not because of the way the football season ended?" Jack said.

"I knew we couldn't go one entire day without talking about the way the football season ended," Teddy said.

It had been an amazing season for the Wildcats, even though they'd lost Jack as the starting quarterback in the first game. But Teddy had switched over from tight end and nearly wrote a storybook ending for himself and for his team. He took the Wildcats all the way down the field and helped get them the lead with just a minute to go in the championship game. But that turned out to be enough time for Scotty Hanley, the Panthers' quarterback. It was just one of those games. Teddy had played great. Gus had caught big passes. But the last team with the ball won, and on the last play, when Scotty hit his tight end for the touchdown that made it 33–32, Panthers. It was another thing you had to appreciate about sports: that you could still love it even after your team lost.

"It was a dream game," Jack said, "until it became kind of a nightmare at the very end."

"You know what *I* dream about doing?" Gus said. "Draining a shot over Scotty to win our first basketball game, right before the buzzer. See how he likes it."

Even though tryouts for their town team, the Warriors, weren't until Saturday, the league schedule had already been posted. And by the luck of the draw, the first game was Walton against Norris.

It was, Gus thought, the best thing about being their age. There was always another season starting, for the guys, and for Cassie, too. She was the point guard for the seventh-grade girls' team, which had gone undefeated last season, same as her softball team had in the spring. The girls' team—the Lady Mustangs, a name she hated—had made things look so easy, rolling through their own league with so many blowout games that she had occasionally threatened to switch to hockey this winter.

"You get around to deciding what sport you're going to play?" Gus said.

"Maybe I have," Cassie said, sounding mysterious, even though there were rarely any mysteries with her, just because she never seemed to hold anything back. "Who knows, maybe you're not the only one who figured something out today."

"Are we allowed to guess?" Teddy said.

"You could," she said, "but you'd be wrong. Like you were wrong thinking you and Teddy had any shot of beating Jack and me at two-on-two."

"You just got lucky in the end," Gus said.

She patted him on the arm. "Go with that," mimicking what he'd said after she picked the teams.

Gus said, "C'mon, you know I just took pity on the girl in the game and let her *think* she'd faked me out on the last play." He leaned back as he said it, from experience, before Cassie could punch him in the arm.

"Yeah," Cassie said. "You never care whether you win or lose."

"We lost because of me," Teddy said to Gus.

Teddy wasn't as good at basketball as he was at either baseball or football. But he had size and good hands and had already proven to them what a fast learner he was in the other sports, now that he'd gotten himself into shape and found out how much he loved competing. It was why his three best friends had been telling him that he definitely ought to try out for the Warriors.

"I'm just not a basketball player," Teddy said now, "no matter how much you guys keep telling me I am."

"Right," Jack said. "Like you weren't a catcher who ended up playing with us in the Little League World Series. Like you weren't a quarterback who nearly won us a championship after I got hurt."

"The way I see it, we need two things to be a championship

team in hoops," Gus said. "We need a little more size up front, and we need a point guard, now that Mike's family is moving."

Mike O'Keeffe had always played all three sports with them, from the time they'd started playing organized sports. But his dad had gotten some big job out in Silicon Valley, and they weren't even waiting until the end of the school year to move.

"You make a good point," Jack said to Gus.

"About point?" Cassie said.

Jack ignored her, as difficult as that was to do sometimes.

"Gus is the best-shooting small forward around," he said. "Steve Kerrigan, as much as I hate to admit it, is stellar at center."

Steve Kerrigan was the son of the mayor, but he was so full of himself that you got the idea he thought *he* was the mayor of Walton. Still, there was no getting around the fact that he was tall and fast and could handle the ball amazingly well for a center. As selfish as he could act off the court, he was unselfish on it. Gus hated to admit it too, but Steve was a star hooper through and through, the best big man in their league by far last season.

Cassie raised an eyebrow. "What about shooting guard?" she said, looking at Jack. "Oh, wait, that would be you."

"I shoot it okay," Jack said.

"Yeah," Gus said, "like Steph Curry shoots it okay."

"I love it when you're modest, Callahan," Cassie said.

"You ever think about trying that, Cass?" Gus said, and moved back fast enough that she only ended up punching air. But she was laughing as she did.

"You know you could play point if you had to," Gus said to Jack. "Being a shoot-first point guard hasn't exactly hurt Steph Curry."

It was funny, he thought, how much more time they spent talking about Steph these days, and not just the four of them. The other night Gus had been watching a Warriors-Spurs game with Gus, and Steph had gotten into the lane and put up one of those underhand floaters of his that just kissed the top of the backboard, and his dad had leaned back and smiled, saying, "*Genio.*"

The Spanish word for "genius."

"I'm better off where I am," Jack said.

"C'mon," Gus said. "You could move to the one if you had to. I could play two."

"Listen to the new Mr. Basketball," Teddy said. "Now he wants to be a player-coach."

"Seriously," Gus said, "with Mike moving away, who *is* going to play point guard for us?"

"That's easy," Cassie Bennett said. "I am."

THREE

"You're joking, right?" Gus said to her.

"Do I look like I'm joking?"

She did not. Gus knew it. He was sure Jack and Teddy knew it too. She had the Look. It was what you saw on her face when she needed a big strikeout in softball, or when she was coming up the court with the basketball in a close game. Or when she was having a disagreement with one of them, about anything, and her basic position was this:

I'm right, and you're pretty much an idiot.

Jack remembered the Look from last baseball season, back when he was helping coach Cassie's team, and she challenged him to get into the batter's box against her. Her face told him everything about how much she wanted to strike him out, and she nearly did, getting two strikes on him before Jack took her deep.

She still hadn't gotten over that. Jack had tried to bring it up a couple of times, trying to make the story funny. But he figured out pretty quickly that Cassie didn't think it was funny, and he never brought it up again.

"What's wrong with your own basketball team?" Gus said. "What about Katie and Gracie and the rest of those guys?"

"Girls," Cassie said.

"You know what I meant," Gus said.

"We won every game last season, the way we did in softball," she said. "I sat out so many fourth quarters, because we were winning by so much, I lost count."

"And, what, winning's getting old for you now?" Teddy said. He sighed and said, "At such a young age, too."

They both knew he was kidding. Teddy Madden, they all knew, thought his sense of humor could stop rain from falling.

"What I've *really* figured out," Cassie said, "is that I need a new challenge. Gus, you know you challenged yourself the first time you played football, just because everybody, at least at the time, thought you were strictly a baseball guy."

"Let me get this straight," Gus said. "You're bored with winning in girls' basketball, so you want to play boys' basketball. Does that mean you're going to give up softball in the spring and come play with us?"

Of all of them, Gus was the least afraid of Cassie Bennett. He didn't take her on all that often, because getting into a debate with her was like having a job. But when he did take her on, he had as little back-up in him as she did.

"Did you ever hear of Mo'ne Davis?" she said.

Everyone their age had heard of Mo'ne Davis, Cassie knew that before she ever asked the question. A couple of summers before, the whole country knew her name. She was the girl who had helped pitch her team from Philadelphia into the Little League World Series, the year before Jack and Gus and Teddy made it to Williamsport.

"You're saying you're her?" Gus said.

"You're saying I'm not?"

There was always this light in Cassie's eyes. Gus's mom told him sometimes that it didn't take much for that light to turn into a fire. Gus could see it happening now.

"Cass," Gus said, "you know I think you're great in sports, no matter how much I joke around with you. Everybody in town knows how great you are."

It was as if Cassie hadn't even heard that. "And by the way?" she said. "A lot of people think Mo'ne is a better basketball player than she is a baseball player. I hear she's a lock to play at UConn someday."

"Men's or women's team?" Gus said.

Suddenly it was as if Jack and Teddy weren't even there. No more two-on-two today. This was Gus and Cassie. One-on-one.

"If Mo'ne Davis could play and *pitch* on a baseball team that could make it to the Little League World Series," Cassie said, "you give me one good reason why you think I shouldn't even be allowed to try out for the Walton Warriors."

Her words were loud in a gym empty except for the four of them. Now it was quiet. Gus used the quiet to think about what he wanted to say next. He really wasn't afraid to tangle with her. Hey, one of them had to man up and do it once in a while. But even knowing her as well as he did, he was surprised to see her fire up this quickly. It was like she'd turned into Mo'ne and was bringing the heat at him.

He took a deep breath, to buy himself a little more time. "I never said you shouldn't be allowed to try out," he said finally. "I just don't think you should want to."

"Why, because you don't think it's a good idea?"

"I didn't say that."

"Sounds like it to me," she said. "Sounds like you might have some kind of prejudice against girls playing on boys' teams, even though it happens all the time. I've read up on it."

Now Gus was the one getting hot. "I'm not prejudiced against anybody," he said. "When your family comes from another country, well, you just aren't."

"I didn't mean it that way."

"Sounded like it."

They were facing each other. The gym was silent again. Gus could hear himself breathing.

"Can I ask you a question?" Gus said.

"Go ahead."

"Would you be doing this to make our team better, or to prove some kind of point?" Gus said.

"Why can't I do both?"

"I think it's more about proving a point to people, starting with us. We all know how you love to show us up in sports if you get the chance. Now it's like you want to show the whole town. And if that's true, then it's not about the team. It's about you."

"And that would make me some kind of bad teammate?"

Gus put his head down and shook it slowly from side to side. He knew how fast her brain worked, and how once you did get into a debate with her, she had this way of getting your own brain all twisted up.

"No!" he said. "You're always the best teammate on your

teams." He paused. "I just honestly wonder if by trying to show everybody, you're going to turn our season into a show."

"What if the point I'm trying to prove is to myself?"

"By saying girls' teams aren't good enough for you anymore?"

She started to say something, but before she could, Teddy finally jumped back in, like he was a boxing announcer. "Ding-ding-ding, end of round three," he said. "Ultimate fighters back to your corners. You first, Ronda Rousey."

"We're not fighting," Cassie said. "We're disagreeing."

"Well, you do know what your mom calls you sometimes: the professional *againster*."

"I never should have told you that," Cassie said.

She still wasn't done. She looked at Gus and said, "Do you seriously not want me to try out for the Warriors?"

"You mean, do I not want you to *make* the Warriors," he said. "You know you will."

"So you're saying I shouldn't do it even though you think I'm good enough to do it?"

"You want me to be honest?" Gus said. "No, I don't think you should do it."

"So it's okay for us to be friends, and to hang out together all the time, and think of ourselves as the home team," she said. "But it's not all right for us to actually *be* on the same team."

"You're going to make it weird," he said.

"One of us is," Cassie Bennett said.

With that she got up and walked out of the gym without looking back, even though her mom was going to be Gus's ride home, and Jack's. When she was through the door and the gym was quiet again, Teddy Madden said, "That went well."

FOUR

Gus knew Cassie wasn't going to change her mind.

Once she dug in on something, you had as much chance of turning her around as you did the Walton River.

Gus thought of Cassie as a sister. He didn't love her the way he did his twin, Angela, maybe because Angela didn't annoy him the way Cassie could, or because Angela just made it so easy to love her and be around her. He and Angela could disagree about stuff. But they didn't fight the way brothers and sisters could sometimes. Gus and Cassie did.

The relationship that Jack and Cassie had was different. They were both stars, or as close to being stars as you could be in the eighth grade. And Jack had a way of dealing with Cassie, somehow focusing on her strengths and doing his best to ignore stuff that could drive Gus crazy. Somehow Jack knew how to pick his spots with her.

It reminded Gus of one of his mom's expressions:

You had to decide which hills were worth fighting for.

But Cassie?

She fought for all of them.

Somehow Gus had managed to get through the rest of the week without talking about basketball—*boys'* basketball—with her, even with them spending as much time together as they always did. He also knew he'd said everything he needed to say, the same as Cassie had. If she felt she'd gotten the last word, it was fine with Gus.

But right up until his dad dropped him off at Walton High School for tryouts, Gus was still holding out hope that Cassie wouldn't show up.

She showed. A few minutes after Gus and Jack got there, Cassie walked through the double doors with Teddy at her side.

All week long, Teddy was the one who kept threatening *not* to show up; who kept saying he didn't want to try out. Even the night before, when Gus was FaceTiming with him, Teddy had said he honestly didn't know whether he'd be there in the morning or not.

"Dude," Gus had said, "you gotta do this."

"Why?"

"Because you belong with us, that's why."

Gus still wasn't sure if he could explain, even to himself, why he thought Cassie didn't belong, why he didn't want a girl on the team, even if she was his good friend. He just told himself to focus on being happy that Teddy was in the gym, even as unhappy as he was that Cassie was with him.

"Just treat her like everybody else," Jack said to him in a quiet voice, as if he could read Gus's mind. "And keep reminding yourself that she's one of your best friends."

"Treat her like everybody else?" Gus said. "Are you insane? This is Cassie we're talking about. She thinks she's better than everybody else!"

"Don't worry about her, is all I'm saying," Jack said. "Worry about yourself. This isn't you against Cassie."

"She didn't have to do this."

"She thinks she does."

"This is going to get messed up, wait and see," Gus said.

"Only if you let it," Jack said. "And only if *we* let it."

He gently pulled Gus by the arm and said, "Now come on."

They walked down to where Cassie and Teddy were standing.

Gus put out a fist so Cassie could bump it. He thought she might have hesitated briefly, but she did it.

"Good luck today," Gus said.

"You too."

"*Hel-lo?*" Teddy said. "I'm here too. And I'm the one who's actually going to need luck."

"Oh yeah," Gus said, grinning at him. "Good luck."

Teddy said, "I recall you being a lot more supportive last week before the Norris game."

"That was for a championship," Gus said. "This is tryouts."

Teddy made a motion like he was wiping sweat off his forehead. "Thanks for clearing that up," he said. "I feel *much* better now."

"All you need to do," Jack said, "is play today the way you play with us."

Cassie nodded. "You've done everything else you set out to do in sports," she said. "Now do this."

"How come whenever you say something like that, in my head I hear you saying 'or else' at the end of the sentence?" Teddy said to her.

"Don't have a bad attitude," she said.

"I'm here, aren't I?" he said. "I don't have a bad attitude. I'm just not as good at basketball as you guys are. And I don't love it as much."

"Love it today," she said, then smiled as she added, "Or else."

There were maybe two dozen kids trying out for a dozen spots on the Warriors. Some kids in their grade had already signed up for the rec league at the Walton YMCA, just because they didn't want to devote the time to travel ball, or because they didn't think they had a realistic shot of making the team. Last year there had been two travel teams from Walton, but the board for Walton Basketball had announced before school even started that there wasn't enough money in the budget for two teams this year, and that the eighth graders not making the Warriors would be placed on rec league teams.

Gus knew that Coach Keith had played high school basketball in Rawson and gone on to be a starter at point guard for the College of Charleston. He had coached a couple of years of eighth-grade ball in Rawson, but the board at Walton had hired him away, because he was supposed to be that good. According to Jack's dad, who was on the board, Coach Keith was probably going to be coaching somewhere in high school next year.

Coach wasn't going to be the only one doing the evaluating today. There were three dads from the board—none with a child trying out—who were going to help him. But everybody knew that Coach's opinion was going to carry the most weight. He was the one who'd had the most success in basketball when he was still a player. If they thought highly enough of him to bring him over from Rawson, he knew the most too.

When it was time to start, he sat the kids in the bleachers, so he could address all of them at once. He was just under six feet tall, Gus guessed, and reminded him of Pharrell Williams, just without the hat.

"Gonna keep this short," he said. "Today is for you guys." He stopped himself then, smiled, and nodded at Cassie, seated between Jack and Teddy. "And girl," he said.

It produced a small laugh in the bleachers. Cassie had been the focus of attention from the time she'd shown up. Gus didn't know how many kids in their class had known she was going to do this. But now everybody knew.

"Play your best today," Coach said. "Play your best, have fun, don't get stuck on any mistakes you make, as if they're going to be the difference between you making this team or not. I'll be more interested in what you do *after* you make a mistake. Because in the end, sports is about overcoming stuff: mistakes, the person guarding you, the other team. Just go out and find your best self out on this court. When you're finished, the dads here and I will try not to make mistakes picking the team."

They broke off then into four groups for what Coach Keith called his "skill drills": dribbling, passing, free-throw shooting, outside shooting, even shooting layups with both hands. They picked the six players in each group alphabetically, so Cassie and Jack ended up together, the way Gus and Teddy did.

Gus was relieved. He wanted to steer clear of Cassie as long as possible. Maybe he wouldn't have to compete against her at all, and he'd be able to do exactly what Jack had told him to do:

Play his game, not Cassie's.

Because Gus truly had come to love this game, more than he ever thought he would. He loved it now, being in this gym, the game all around him, guys moving and passing and shooting. Gus even loved the sound of it, the bounce of the ball and Coach Keith's whistle blowing from time to time. They hadn't even started scrimmaging yet, but when they did, they would all sense the same thing: this was the real team game, five players, one ball. So often all five players would get to touch the ball, sometimes more than once when the ball was being shared and the game was being played the way it was supposed to be. Gus's father had told him that even though baseball was a team game too, it was so different from basketball, because in baseball it didn't really matter if the left fielder knew the catcher's name. Gus knew the relationship between a pitcher and catcher, or shortstop and second baseman, was different. But he understood what his dad meant.

Football? Gus was a wide receiver, so he knew what football could be like. Sometimes he felt as if his teammates were playing the game without him, especially when the ball wasn't being thrown in his direction.

Basketball was different. You filled open spaces. You moved yourself and the ball. You tried to get open. And you tried to find the open man. Then you went to the other end of the court and tried to stop the other team from doing all the good things you'd just done.

Before long they *were* scrimmaging, first two half-court games of four-on-four, with subs. Then they were finally play-ing real ball, five-on-five, full court, running some simple plays, setting picks, fast-breaking when they got the chance, almost like they were watching the season begin to take shape in front of their eyes.

Gus thought of another Spanish word his dad used when he talked about basketball.

Belleza.

A beauty.

FIVE

It turned out Gus was as hot as he'd been in the gym at Walton Middle playing two-on-two with his friends. Steph Curry and Klay Thompson of the Warriors had been nicknamed the Splash Brothers. This morning, Gus felt like one of them. In the modern language of the game, his shot was wet. It reached the point where he was surprised when one of his shots *didn't* drop.

During a break, Jack came over to him and demanded a high

five. When Gus tried to give him one with his right hand, Jack shook his head.

"Shooting hand, please," he said. "Whatever you've got going, I want some of it to rub off on me."

"You're doing just fine," Gus said.

"I'm fine," Jack Callahan said. "But you're unconscious."

"If that's true," Gus said, "don't wake me up until we're done."

The last scrimmage included guys Gus was pretty sure would make the team, off what he knew from having played with most of them, and also what he'd seen them doing today: Jack, Jake Mozdean, Max Conte, Brian McAuley, Henry Koepp. All had played both baseball and football.

Steve Kerrigan was out there too, a head taller than anybody else at tryouts. He'd been one of the best players on their sixth-grade team and had gotten even better by the time they were in seventh. Over the last year, Gus was sure the guy had grown six more inches. He was the kid their age who had no interest in playing other sports; he just focused on basketball. When Jack and Gus were playing baseball in the summer, Steve was attending one fancy basketball camp after another, even as far away as California. There was no doubt in Gus's mind that he could hold his own at any of them.

Gus wished he liked Steve more. But he didn't. It wasn't just that he was the mayor's son and acted as if that made him royalty in Walton. He also seemed to think that because he was so good at basketball, it allowed him to treat people like dirt. And when Steve would get called out, he was one of those guys who said, *Hey, I was just kidding around, don't be so sensitive.*

As cocky as Cassie could be, and as annoying sometimes, she seemed as humble as Jack when you compared her to Steve Kerrigan, whom Gus did call Mayor Kerrigan to Jack and Cassie and Teddy.

There were two other players who made it to the last scrimmage:

Teddy Madden.

Cassie Bennett.

When Gus hadn't been on the court, he'd been trying to keep an eye on both of them, and he knew that Cassie had had been doing more than holding her own. But Teddy had been having a tougher time. He could rebound and was a legit defender, as long as the guy he was guarding wasn't too quick. But he couldn't put the ball on the floor to save his life, and he was struggling to get his own shot, even in close to the basket.

It was different with Cassie.

From the first time she was out there playing four-on-four in the half-court games, she played as if she belonged. If she was nervous, she wasn't showing it. Maybe she didn't get nervous, even when she was the only girl in the game.

Now Coach Keith put her with Steve, Teddy, Max Conte, and Wayne Coffey. Gus had Jack with him, Brian McAuley, Len Ritchie—who was almost as big as Steve and was probably going to be their backup center—and Henry, who'd backed up Jack last season at shooting guard. Knowing the strengths and weaknesses of everybody out there, Gus thought the sides were as even as they could be. He told himself to play as if *this* was the first game of the season, and show Coach that he was more than just a shooter, that he was a *player.*

"Now, Gustavo," Steve Kerrigan said to him before they started. "I don't want you to get distracted because there's a girl playing point guard for our team. By the way, I can never keep it straight: Is she your girl, or Jack's?"

"Her own," Gus said, and knelt down to tie his shoes, as a way of ending the conversation. Steve Kerrigan had never forgotten that Gus's full name was Gustavo. Somehow when he used it—and he used it a lot—it always sounded to Gus like Steve was making fun of him, or insulting him. Gus thought about addressing him as Mayor Kerrigan, but what was the point?

Why would *he* want to act like a jerk?

When he stood up, Steve hadn't moved away from him.

"Your game has certainly improved," he said to Gus. "I'd

MIKE LUPICA

always thought that coming from where you come from, baseball was your game."

"You mean coming from the west side of Walton?" Gus said, and walked over to where Jack was standing a few feet away.

"Heard what he said," Jack said. "His game's improved too. But his attitude hasn't."

"I'm not letting him get under my skin."

"Try to do the same thing with the other team's point guard."

"You mean the girl?" Gus said, as if he hadn't noticed.

After Coach Keith put twenty minutes up on the scoreboard clock, it turned into a good game. There were no set plays, but because so many of the kids on the floor had played together before, they remembered basic stuff from the previous season, about high pick-and-rolls being a good way to start any offense, about ball sharing, and spacing, and movement.

"Wait a second," Coach called out after Jack hit Gus with a sweet pass off a pick-and-roll and Gus ended up with a layup. "This team may be able to coach itself this season!"

Gus hit a few more shots from the outside after that. Jack hit a long three-pointer. Len Ritchie even picked up a couple of put-backs off offensive rebounds. They were pretty much dealing on offense. That wasn't an issue. The issue was that Cassie and Steve Kerrigan were dealing at the other end as if they'd been playing together their whole lives.

Even Gus had to admit to himself that it was something to see.

If you didn't know basketball, you wouldn't have thought she was doing anything outstanding. Or flashy. By the time it was 16–11 for her team, she hadn't scored a single basket. But if you *did* know the game, you realized she kept making the right pass, usually to Steve and usually in a place where he could do something once he had the ball in his hands. Brian McAuley was doing a good job of covering her, making her work, never giving her enough room to even think about putting up an outside shot. But Gus knew that if any of the dads were keeping unofficial stats, she was piling up assists. She even managed to get Teddy a layup.

And for once, she wasn't doing any talking. She barely looked at either Gus or Jack. Gus kept waiting for her to give him some kind of look, just one, to let him know that *she* knew how well she was doing with—and against—the boys. But it never came. She was all business, the same as he was. For these few moments, they were nothing more than opponents, both trying to get a W.

When Coach Keith gave them a time-out with one minute left, it was 22–21 for what Gus was actually thinking of as Cassie's team.

"You know she's loving every minute of this," Gus said in

a quiet voice to Jack as they were drinking water out of the bottles they'd brought.

"She's about to make this team," Jack said. "Nothing for her *not* to love."

"What about Teddy?" Gus said.

Cassie had just faked a pass to Steve and hit Teddy for what should have been an easy layup. But he shot it way too hard off the backboard before Steve Kerrigan grabbed the rebound and cleaned up with a layup of his own.

Jack made a shaky motion with his hand.

On their next possession, he set a pick for Gus at the other end, Brian threw Gus the ball in the corner, and he made another shot from there. Cassie came down and got Steve one more open look, but he missed a wide-open eight-footer. Teddy, though, was there to clean up for him and bank the ball home.

Their team was back up by a point.

With twenty seconds left, Jack ended up with the ball on the left side, calmly dribbling as he checked the clock. This was the big moment of the game, last-shot time, his team down by a point. Jack had always been a big-moment guy, in any sport he'd ever played.

It didn't mean Jack was going to *take* the last shot. But he was going to find the best shot for his team. Jack always talked about playing the right way. If Gus was sure of anything, he was sure that Jack would do that now, even in a scrimmage. All that ever mattered to Jack was if somebody was keeping score.

Gus felt himself smiling as he watched Jack and watched the clock himself. Somehow, Jack having the ball made Gus feel as if they were ahead and not behind.

With twelve seconds left, Brian suddenly sprinted over and set a pick for Jack on Wayne Coffey, who'd been guarding Jack for most of the scrimmage.

Cassie switched.

She was covering Jack now.

Eight seconds left.

Jack crossed over on her, going to his right-hand dribble, heading for the free-throw line. As he did, Gus flashed across and set *another* pick, a legal one, even though Cassie didn't see him coming. But he made sure to give her enough room, so Coach wouldn't blow a whistle and call him for a blocking foul.

Cassie, focused on staying with Jack, never saw him. Nobody on her team called out the screen. She ran into Gus so hard he could hear the air come out of her, and she went down. Hard. Jack blew past both of them for the layup that won the game for their team by a point.

Gus put a hand down to help Cassie up.

"Sorry about that," he said.

"Are you?" she said, but gave him a small smile as she allowed him to pull her to her feet.

"C'mon," he said. "You know I am."

"Would you have apologized for putting a guy on the floor?" she said.

Gus shook his head. "The game's over," he said. "You can stop grinding now." He put out his fist again, the way he had when she'd walked into the gym. She tapped his with hers. "Good game," he said.

"You too."

They stood there looking at each other, almost like they were strangers in that moment, then walked off the court in different directions, like they really were on different teams, even though they were about to be on the same one.

SIX

Cassie made the team.

Teddy did not.

As strange as things had gotten between Gus and Cassie since she'd made her announcement about trying out for the Warriors, they still all got together at Jack's house the next day, knowing that the roster was supposed to be posted on the town's basketball website at noon.

When it was, when they saw Cassie's name right at the top of the list because they'd done it alphabetically and then didn't see Teddy's down below, they all turned and looked at him. Nobody knew what to say.

So of course Teddy spoke first.

"Guys," he said, "it's okay. If you guys hadn't pressured me so much, I'm not sure I would have tried out in the first place. So stop looking at me like my dog ran away."

Gus grinned, knowing Teddy was trying to make this easier on everybody.

"Which would be even sadder if you *had* a dog," he said.

"Besides," Teddy said, "I've got a backup plan. Actually, it was my original plan until it had to become a backup because you were all delusional enough to think I was good enough to play travel basketball."

"Are you going to tell us?" Jack said.

"I'm going to ask Coach Keith if I can be manager," Teddy said. "I'll still get to hang around with you losers while you try to win games."

Then he put up his hand, so she could hit him with a high five. "Way to go, Cass," he said. "You made history."

"I just wanted to make the team," she said. "But I wanted you to make it too."

"I tried to tell you guys I wasn't good enough," Teddy said. "It would've been cool for all four of us to be on the same team. But three will do."

"Okay, then," Gus said. "Three of us against the world it is."

"You sure it's not going to be us against each other?" Cassie said.

"No, Cass, it's not," he said.

He looked over at Jack and Teddy.

"Help me out here," he said. "Haven't we already talked this thing to death?"

Teddy grinned. "Well, in Cassie's case, isn't it talking things *until* death?"

She said, "Have I ever mentioned you're not as funny as you think you are?"

"On multiple occasions," he said.

Jack got up and stood in front of the television, making it feel as if he were talking to all of them at once, because he really was.

"Listen," he said. "Cassie, you know there's no better teammate in the world than Gus. Or better friend. Not even you. And now that we are all on the same team, there's no way he's *not* gonna support you the way he supports the guys on the team."

"I think what Jack is saying," Teddy said, "is that you're officially one of the boys now. Something you've aspired to pretty much your whole life."

Without even looking, like it was a no-look pass on the court, she reached over and pinched him.

"Ow?" he said.

"Now who's a girl?" she said.

Mrs. Callahan called down from upstairs and said lunch was ready. Gus started to head for the stairs. Cassie blocked his path.

"You're sure this isn't going to be a thing?" she said.

"Only if we have to talk about it every single day from now until the end of the season!" he said.

"I still don't understand why this bothers you."

"If I figure it out," Gus said, "you'll be the first to know, I promise."

At halftime of the Packers-Patriots game they were watching, Aaron Rodgers against Tom Brady, number 12 against number 12, Jack wanted to know who was up for a quick game of two-on-two basketball in his driveway. Cassie and Teddy said they were in, and Teddy pointed out that it would be fun playing no-stress basketball again. But Gus begged off, saying he had homework to finish.

"Wait a second," Jack said. "You're saying you're *not* going to watch football and you *can't* play hoops—even though it's warm enough to do that outside—because of *school*?"

"Who are you," Teddy said, "and what have you done with our friend Gus Morales?"

"My mom is on me big-time, I swear," Gus said. "After the

teacher conferences the other day, she came home and lit me up because all the teachers said pretty much the same thing: not only could I be doing better, I *should* be doing better."

"I thought that's what every teacher has said at every teacher conference since the beginning of time," Cassie said. "I think it's some kind of rule they passed."

"Anyway," Gus said, "I promised her I would work harder. And if I work harder on a Sunday, I can score some huge points with her."

"I like it," Teddy said, and informed the group that he was going home and trying the same thing.

Before Gus and Teddy left the basement, Cassie said to Gus, "So we're good?"

"We're good," he said, and followed Teddy up the stairs.

He knew this girl. The longer they stayed together today, the more she was going to want to start talking about the whole thing—and whether or not it really *was* a thing—all over again. It was like another rule that somebody had passed, but just for girls, whether they were friends or sisters or moms. They really did want to talk things to death, or until death, as if talking could solve all the world's problems. Gus didn't think guys—with the possible exception of Teddy—were wired like that. He knew he wasn't.

Gus rode home on his bike, taking his time. He wasn't lying

about homework, or about the way his mom had gotten on his case after the conferences. He was going to get busy with history and English, the two classes he liked the best and wanted to do better in, when he got home. But he just needed some air. He needed to be alone. As he rode along, he realized how happy he was with the quiet, and he tried to use it to understand what he'd told Cassie he didn't.

But there was one person who might:

His twin sister, Angela.

Even with a good wind in his face, Gus felt himself smiling, thinking how much it would crush Cassie if he ever told her that she wasn't the smartest girl he knew.

Angela Morales was.

SEVEN

She was in her room, on her bed, staring at the screen of her laptop, as if by staring hard enough she might be able to unlock the secrets of the universe. Or maybe just learn some things that would make her even smarter than she already was.

Angela was like that. It was like she really was studying the universe the way most kids their age just studied for quizzes or tests or made their fantasy teams better.

In addition to being Gus's sister, she was also one of Cassie

Bennett's best girlfriends at school. When Cassie wasn't hanging with Gus and Jack and Teddy, she was with Angela, or Katie Cummings, or Gracie Zaro. But Angela never traveled in a pack. There were too many other kids in their class, boys and girls, she found interesting. There were too many things for her to do. Even in the eighth grade, Angela liked to watch the news on television.

She was shaking her head as Gus walked in. From downstairs they could smell their mom's cooking. Sometimes the big family meal on Sunday was lunch. It would be dinner today, because Gus had been at Jack's at lunchtime.

"This Mayor Kerrigan," she said, "is not a nice man."

"Still not too crazy about his son, either," Gus said. "He was giving me that 'Gustavo' stuff at tryouts yesterday."

"It's a way for him to disrespect you and our family," she said. When she looked up at him, he could see that her face was flushed, the way it got when she was angry. "He must get it from his father, the hater."

Mayor Stuart Kerrigan had just been reelected a few weeks before. During the campaign, according to Gus's parents and Angela, who'd actually followed it, he was another politician who made immigrants, or even the children of immigrants, sound like they were the devil. One of his big campaign slogans had been:

This is still our town.

Gus's dad had said Mr. Kerrigan used the slogan because there had been a rise in the Hispanic population in Walton over the past few years and because he had been running against a local lawyer named Michael Ruiz. Mr. Ruiz's parents had escaped from Cuba when he was a boy, and he had moved to Walton after graduating from law school.

Gus's dad had added, "I'm surprised the mayor doesn't change the name of our town to Wall-ton. Then he'd really sound like one of those politicians who wants to build a wall around America."

Angela nodded, not looking angry now, just sad.

"It's good Mommy and Daddy got to this country when they did," she said. "Mayor Kerrigan doesn't sound as if anybody in our family would be welcome now."

She closed her laptop. "But you didn't come in here so we could talk about politics, did you, brother?"

"Does Cassie count?"

"She made the team."

"You know?"

"Are you kidding? She Insta-ed a picture of the roster. I think even people in outer space know she made the Warriors by now."

"I just left her," Gus said. "She's pretty proud of herself."

He sat in the chair at Angela's desk, turned it around so he was facing his sister, and saw her smiling.

MIKE LUPICA

"When isn't she?" Angela said. "But we both know who she is. And we both still love her as a friend."

"True."

"So you really can't be surprised that she not only wanted to do this, but that she *has* done this."

"Totally," Gus said. "I would've been shocked if she didn't make it."

"But you still have a problem with this."

"Don't you?" he said. "Her making our team is only going to hurt *your* team."

"I'll survive," she said. "I'm not like Cassie. Or Jack or Teddy or you. Oh, don't get me wrong, brother, I love to play. But when it comes to sports, I'm just not like you guys. I'm mostly out there to have fun and be with my friends."

"So it doesn't bother you that by doing this she's saying your team isn't good enough for her anymore?"

Angela laughed now. She had their mom's laugh, which made Gus think that even the neighbors could hear her.

"This is Cassie we're talking about! She probably doesn't think the Warriors in the NBA are good enough for her!"

"Well, she's my teammate now, and not yours," Gus said. "Whether I like it or not."

"Emphasis on *not*." Angela tilted her head, as if curious. "So what really is bothering you about this? Is it because she's a girl?"

"Will you get mad if I say yes?"

"No."

"Yes!"

She laughed again. It made him feel better. Just talking to her could make him feel better.

"This isn't funny," he said.

"It's not funny, but you are," she said. "You can't let this ruin your season. You can't even let on to Cassie that it's still bothering you."

"But she knows it is."

"I know she knows."

"She said something to you?"

"Of course," she said. "She talks to me like I'm her sister too. And what's bothering her the most is that she does know it's bothering you."

"But why does it?"

It came out of him much louder than he expected, to the point where their mom called up and asked if everything was all right up there.

When Angela spoke to Gus again, her voice was soft. "If I tell you something, *you* promise not to get mad?"

"Promise."

"Twin to twin?"

It was sacred to them, another part of the bond they shared, something deeper, Gus knew, than the fact that they had been born seconds apart.

"Twin to twin," he said, and patted his heart a couple of times to seal the deal the way they always did.

"Okay, here goes," his sister said. She paused just slightly and said, "I think you have always been a little jealous of Cassie, and I think her making your team just makes you even more jealous."

As soon as she said it, Gus was relieved, because he knew she was right.

"But I really shouldn't have any reason to be jealous."

"People don't always need a good reason, brother."

"I've never needed to be the star," Gus said. "Cassie wants to be the star of everything. Jack can't help himself from being a star."

"I think there's more to it than that," Angela said.

"There has to be more to it?"

"Yes," she said. "I think you have always thought of yourself, our whole family, as being outsiders, because of where we come from."

"Oh, come on," he said. "You just have Mayor Kerrigan on the brain, because of all that Wall-ton stuff."

"No," she said, "I'm right about this, too. I feel the same things myself sometimes when I look at Cassie and Jack. They're always going to be more *of* this place than we are."

"Dad says we're as much a part of this town as anybody

else," Gus said. "And just as American, even though we're Dominican American."

His sister gave him a long look. "But do you believe that?"

"I don't know what I believe anymore," he said. "I thought we were talking about Cassie and me being on the same team now."

"We are," she said, "because you guys *are* on the same team. It's why there's something I want you to do for me."

"What's that?"

"Actually, I want to give you some advice from Cassie when a problem comes up," she said. *"Deal!"*

"And stop worrying about a girl being on a boys' team."

"Yeah," Angela said. "Pretty soon girls are going to think they can grow up to be president or something."

"You're saying that you're not even bothered a little bit that she's blown off your team?"

"I never said that," Angela said. "But Cassie and I will figure it out, the same as you and Cassie will. Because guess what? I don't think this is as much of a boy-girl thing as it is a Cassie-Gus thing."

She flipped up the screen of her laptop and made a motion with her hand, waving him out of her room.

"Go play the season," she said.

He went back to his own room and closed the door and

turned out the lights and lay down on his bed. It was the way he did his best thinking.

What he hadn't admitted to Angela was how much this whole thing with Cassie was ripping him up inside. He knew how good a friend she was. He knew how hard he had always rooted for her in sports, and how hard she had rooted for him. He knew she had earned her way onto the team. He knew she had shown everybody in the gym that she was good enough to play with the boys.

But as far as he could tell, it was only bothering one boy:

Him.

In a family where the parents had always preached tolerance, and Gus and Angela had been taught to practice tolerance, Gus knew he was being *intolerant* about Cassie playing for the Warriors. Even if it didn't hurt the team in the end, he knew it was hurting their friendship.

He knew how much that was burning him up inside, as hard as he tried not to let it show. He just didn't know how to make that go away. He knew he should just try to accept her, and accept that they were teammates, and move on. But that was easier said than done.

I have to try harder, he told himself in the quiet and dark of his room.

Maybe tryouts weren't over after all.

EIGHT

As excited as Gus was to get another shot at the Norris Panthers, even though this was a different sport, he knew he was more excited because it was opening day. Opening day was always special in sports. To Gus, it was like opening up a good book, one you really wanted to read, and not knowing where it was going to take you, or how it was going to come out.

While both teams were warming up, right before they got into their layup lines, Gus and Jack stood with Scotty Hanley at half court. Teddy Madden, on his first official day as team manager, was there, too, brand-new scorebook in hand.

"You know we owe you one, right?" Gus said.

Scotty grinned. "I was afraid of that," he said.

"What do you mean we owe him *one*?" Teddy said, stepping hard on the last word.

"Aw, come on, dude," Scotty said. "We just got lucky at the end of the championship game, ending up with the ball last."

"Our plan," Jack said, "is to get lucky like that today."

Scotty said, "Hey, how cool would it be if we ended up playing for the championship in hoops, too?"

"Yeah," Gus said. "Us playing and you watching."

Scotty quickly high-fived them all and told them to have a good one. They told him to do the same. As Scotty walked away, Teddy said, "I'd love to hate him. But he's a really good dude."

"A really good dude about to have his day be totally ruined," Gus said.

They hadn't noticed Cassie come up behind them. She was wearing number 3, just because Chris Paul of the Clippers was her favorite NBA player. He was nicknamed CP3. Some guys on the team were already calling Cassie CB3.

"You good?" Gus said to her.

Cassie said, "Hope so."

"Do I detect doubt from our friend Cassie Bennett, the queen of the world?" Teddy said.

"You already showed Coach you *can* play," Gus said. "No way you won't play."

Look at me, he thought. *Captain Positive.*

But he really was trying to be positive, by being the best teammate to her he could be, not letting his feelings about Cassie being in the game and not in the stands, where he honestly felt she belonged, get in the way of trying to win the game. It was a piece of advice that Gus's dad stressed constantly:

The key to doing your best in sports started with getting out of your own way.

The Panthers had the same starting five they'd had for seventh-grade ball, Gus noticed: Scotty at shooting guard; David Bicknell, another good dude, at point guard; Sam Kennedy at center. Their small forward, whom Gus would be guarding, was Alonzo McRae, crushing some cool cornrows this year. Billy Young was their power forward.

Coach Keith went with Gus, Jack, Steve Kerrigan at center, Max Conte at power forward, Brian McAuley at point. Jake Mozdean would be their first guy off the bench, because he was a perfect swingman, able to play almost any position on the court.

Coach Keith got them around him in a circle right before the game started and said, "I'm going to tell you the same boring stuff I tell you every day at practice. If you're open, shoot. If somebody else is open, pass the ball and let them shoot. Don't back up for one second. Make sure you have your teammates' backs. And have fun. If I think you aren't having fun, I'll put somebody else in the game I think will."

He put his hand out. They put theirs on top of it. "Go Warriors," he said.

"*Go Warriors!*" they yelled back at him, like they were trying to rattle the backboards, or just raise the roof.

The ref with the ball blew his whistle. "Oh, and one more thing," Coach Keith said. "If anybody gives us a hard time because of Bennett"—it was what he called her—"or gives her a hard time, there is only one response from this team, including Bennett. We don't answer back, except to get the next bucket, or the next stop. There's all sorts of ways to be better than the other team in sports."

But the Norris Panthers were better early.

By a lot.

In the first quarter it was the Panthers doing all the things that Coach always preached: sharing the ball, filling open spaces, filling up the basket when you got an open look. By the time the buzzer sounded ending the quarter, they were up ten points, and it could have been worse than that.

Every Panthers player on the court had at least one basket by then, and Gus knew exactly where that started: with their point guard, David Bicknell. It wasn't that he was dominating Brian, or even making Brian look that bad. He was just getting the ball to his teammates where they could do something with it. Maybe you had to be in the game to notice it. Gus wasn't sure that even people in the stands noticed it. But David always seemed to be a half step ahead of Brian, and sometimes in basketball, that was all it took.

Coach subbed in Jake for Max at the start of the second quarter, because Jake had already shown Coach, just in the first week of practices, that he could be an instant-offense guy off the bench. But even Jake was off, missing his first two shots. Gus had made his first two shots of the game but hadn't scored since. Three minutes into the second quarter, the Panthers' lead had grown to sixteen.

Coach called time and subbed in Cassie for Brian.

"Don't try to do too much," Coach said to her in the huddle. "We're not going to make this up all at once. I'd rather slow things down a bit, run our stuff, run some clock when we've got the ball. Make *them* chase a little bit. If we do, I guarantee this will be a game by halftime."

They made it a game by halftime. Gus made a three-pointer, his first of the year. Jack made a couple of outside shots. But the way they really began to wear down the Panthers was when Cassie started pounding the ball inside to Steve Kerrigan, who didn't have a big size advantage over Sam Kennedy, but did have a big talent advantage. They would work the ball around on the outside, Cassie and Jack and Gus looking like they were playing a three-man game, until Steve got open again inside. Then he'd get a layup or short jumper or even his new baby hook.

The Panthers' coach, Scotty's dad, called a time-out with ninety seconds left in the half. As the Warriors walked over to their bench, Steve put his arm around Gus's shoulders, like they were a couple of old pals. Sometimes Gus thought Steve went through life acting as if there was a TV camera on him.

"Gustavo," he said, "I believe we're now in business."

By now they had cut the Panthers' lead to six, 30–24. Steve had made the Warriors' last four baskets, all coming after passes from Cassie.

"You know," Gus said, taking a big step so that Steve's hand came off him, "it's okay if you call me Gus once in a while."

"Just keeping it real," Steve said, "using your real name."

The Panthers ended up with the last shot of the half. They were the ones working the ball around on the outside now, until Cassie anticipated a crosscourt pass from Alonzo to David Bicknell, stole it cleanly, and took off like a streak of light. Gus saw her give a quick look at the clock behind their basket, to make sure she had enough time to go all the way in for a layup.

Slowing up just that much gave Alonzo, the fastest kid in the game, a chance to catch her from behind.

As Cassie went up with her right hand, Alonzo took a big swing at her and at the ball. A lot of it was probably frustration at his pass being picked off. Or maybe it was because a girl had picked it off. But not only did he knock the ball away, he also knocked Cassie down, hard.

Gus was the Warrior closest to the play. In that moment, everything that had been happening between him and Cassie disappeared. All he could see was her on the ground.

"Hey!" he yelled at Alonzo. "What was that?"

Alonzo was reaching down to help Cassie up. But now he straightened up and wheeled on Gus, because everybody in the gym had heard what Gus said to him.

Jack was next to Gus now. In a voice as soft as Gus's had been loud, Jack said, "Dial it down."

But Gus wasn't done with Alonzo McRrae just yet.

"You weren't playing the ball," he said. "Just her."

"I don't know what you all are taught," Alonzo said. "But we're taught that if you're going to foul on a layup, don't let the shooter get the ball to the iron. 'Less the shooter is a girl, maybe."

The refs got between Gus and Alonzo, telling them both to cut the chatter and walk away.

It turned out to be Cassie, back on her feet, who spoke next. To Gus.

"I don't need protecting," she said, as if she was angrier at Gus than she was at the guy who'd just put her down.

"Listen to her," Alonzo said. "Girl knows what she's talking about."

Her head snapped around. "Oh, shut up," she said.

His eyes got big. "Who's telling me to shut up?"

"I am," she said. "Unless I'm going too fast for you."

The refs waved Gus and Jack and Cassie back to their bench. Alonzo walked back to his, still eyeballing Gus over his shoulder. The two refs got together and decided it wasn't a flagrant foul, that it was a shooting foul: two free throws for Cassie, three seconds showing on the clock.

Now the refs waved both teams back on the court and motioned to Cassie to come get the ball. As she headed to the free-throw line, Gus walked on one side of her, Jack on the other.

"Don't ever do that again," she said, her voice not much more than a whisper, not even looking at Gus as she spoke.

"What, stick up for you?" he said.

"No," she said. "Don't act like I can't take care of myself."

She ran the last few steps toward the ref, who handed her the ball as players from both teams took their places on both sides of the lane. Before Gus joined them, he turned to Jack and said, "Hard to win with her."

"Yeah," Jack said, "but that's exactly what we've got to do in the second half. Win *with* her."

Cassie knocked down both of her shots. They were down four.

They were all into it now, players from both teams. Gus could see it, and feel it, all around him when the second half started. This felt like more than opening day now. They were into the season, big-time. Jack had told Gus to dial it down after Alonzo fouled Cassie. But maybe it was that play that had dialed everything *up*.

Coach Keith went with his starting five to start the third quarter. But when the Panthers got on a rip halfway through and stretched their lead back to eight, he put Cassie in for Brian and Wayne Coffey in at power forward for Max Conte. Gus, who'd been replaced for the last couple of minutes by Jake, went back in with them.

"Let's go back to playing inside out, the way we did when we got back into this thing," Coach said. "Let's pound our big guy. If they try to double on him, he can throw it back out to Jack or Gus."

As they broke the huddle, Jack said to Cassie, "Just like we're playing in my driveway, or yours."

"What about mine?" Gus said.

"Yours too," Jack said.

Cassie stopped and looked at both of them. Gave them the Look. "No," she said. "It's not just us. I have to show everybody I belong."

"Hey, Cass," Gus said. "How about we just show we're the better team?"

He almost added that it wasn't all about her. But he didn't. Even thought that was exactly what he was thinking.

NINE

Cassie didn't play as well now as she had in the first half, mostly because she was trying to do too much, forcing the action, even forcing up a couple of shots when she clearly should have passed.

It was like she had *decided* she was going to be the MVP today.

Coach took her out to start the fourth quarter, but then Brian McAuley, who'd gotten himself into foul trouble in the third quarter, committed two dumb fouls, and fouled out. Gus was secretly hoping that Coach would put Jack at point and move Gus into Jack's spot at shooting guard.

But he went back to Cassie.

The Panthers were doubling Steve now, and because of that, both Gus and Jack were open. Each of them started to make shots, Scott and the Panthers went cold, and when Gus made his second three-pointer of the game, it was 48–all, two minutes left. The game was tied for the first time since 2–2. The Warriors had come all the way back.

Scotty missed a jumper. Jack got the rebound and made a fast outlet pass to Cassie, who threw it back to Jack. Scotty had been slow getting back on defense, and so had everybody else on the Panthers. Jack took the ball all the way to the basket. Now the Warriors were ahead.

Maybe it *was* going to be like football. Maybe the last team with the ball was going to win here, too.

Scotty, who'd made all the plays he had to in football, came right back, stepped back, and made a three. Panthers ahead by one. Fifty seconds left. Jack set a great screen for Gus, Steve passed the ball out to him, Gus knocked down the shot. Warriors by one. But David Bicknell blew by Cassie at the other end, she turned her head because she thought he was going to pass to Scotty, and David got an easy layup.

Fifteen seconds left. Norris was ahead 53–52.

Warriors' ball.

Coach Keith called time.

"We take our first, best shot," he said. "That will be the one that wins us the game."

Jack threw it in to Cassie and immediately ran and set the kind of back screen for Gus in the right corner that he'd been setting since they first started playing ball together. Gus ran free along the baseline and found himself wide open in the other corner.

He checked the clock.

Ten seconds left.

"Cass!" Gus called to her.

This time it was David Bicknell, guarding Cassie at the top of the circle, who turned his head, giving Cassie a step on him. She was at the free-throw line now, with some space, nobody between her and Gus. All she had to do was throw him the ball. Sam Kennedy had stayed home on Steve Kerrigan to Cassie's left. When she saw a lane for herself on the right, she decided to take it.

Five seconds.

Gus checked the clock, then checked Cassie, two steps ahead of David Bicknell, flying to the basket, putting the ball up with two seconds to go.

Sam Kennedy, who didn't have Steve Kerrigan's length but

who sure had enough in that moment, swatted her shot into the stands. Gus watched it come down in the area where some of Cassie's girlfriends were sitting.

Game over.

The Norris Panthers had beaten them by a point, again.

Sometimes you didn't get to be MVP, no matter how much you wanted to be.

Jack was standing in the corner with Gus, who felt like he was still waiting for Cassie to pass him the ball. Cassie ran right over to them, as if she needed to explain herself.

"Coach said take our best shot," Cassie said. "I thought it was a layup."

"Our best shot," Gus said, "or yours?"

"What's that supposed to mean?"

She had a way of doing that, in almost all circumstances, finding a way to turn defense into offense.

"It means," Gus said, "that you wanted to be the open man so much that you convinced yourself you were."

"I was open."

"Not enough," Gus said.

Cassie turned to Jack, as if she thought she might have a better chance with him.

"Do you think that too?"

But before Jack got a chance to answer—before he was forced to answer her—Coach Keith had walked over and told them to go get in the handshake line. When they'd finished with that, he gathered his players in the corner of the gym closest to their bench.

"First of all," he said, "that was a great game we just played, and I want you all to know that I saw so many positives from our team I don't know where to start."

Teddy handed him the score book that he'd kept for the game, and Coach studied it for a moment before saying, "We out-rebounded them and had fewer turnovers. Stats like that, believe me, are going to win us a lot of games this season."

Even after just one tryout and three practices, Gus already knew that Coach Keith could find positives in a power outage. He smiled. "Did we all want a different outcome? Of course we did. But the thing I liked the best today was the way we fought. And as an old coach of mine once said, 'That's not nothing.'"

Then he said he'd see them all Monday night. Gus walked back to the bench to get his Gatorade bottle. Cassie walked right along with him.

"Are we done?" Cassie said.

"Yeah, Cass, we're done for now," he said. "Coach just talked about how hard we fought. But I don't want to fight with you."

"You started it."

Gus stopped. "No," he said. "*You* started it. You're the one who told Jack and me that you were fixed on showing everybody you belonged."

"And you're saying that's why we lost the game?"

"Would you mind lowering your voice?" he said. "The show's over now."

"It wasn't a show," she said. "It was a game I wanted to win as badly as you did."

"Didn't say you didn't."

"It sounds like you're calling me a selfish player."

Gus really did want this to be over. He wanted to go get with Jack and Teddy and get out of here. But he was tired of backing down to Cassie Bennett. And he knew he was right about the way the game had ended.

"You were today," he said.

As soon as he did, he saw the hurt look on her face. But he wasn't backing down. Or taking it back.

"So that's it?" she said.

"Yeah," Gus said. "I guess it is."

He could see that she couldn't just leave it there. She never just left things. But before she could say one more thing, and maybe even get the last word, they both heard Steve Kerrigan.

"Is there a problem, Gooos-tavo?" he said.

Sometimes he dragged out the name, mostly for his own

entertainment. Gus turned, feeling more tired now than he had when the game ended.

"No," he said, "no problem except the final score."

It was almost as if Steve didn't hear him, or didn't care. He turned to Cassie instead.

"Don't worry about the way it ended, Cassie," he said. "You were just trying to make a play."

Gus didn't know if Steve had overheard them. Maybe he didn't know the amount of tension there was between Gus and Cassie these days. Maybe he did.

Maybe Cassie had told him.

"Hey, we're all on the same team, right?" Steve said.

"Right," Gus said.

Right, he thought. *We're just one big happy family right now.*

There was nothing else to say, to either one of them, so he just walked away. Cassie stayed with Steve. He could see them walking in the opposite direction, Cassie talking away now, Steve nodding his head.

When he went to get his bag, Teddy said, "You want to hang out? Though I may need a little rest. Keeping all those stats can wear a guy out."

"Maybe later," Gus said.

"Hey," Teddy said, "it was just one game."

"Was it?" Gus said.

MIKE LUPICA

TEN

Gus took off his uniform as soon as he got home and changed into his sweats. Then he grabbed his basketball and headed for the small court his dad had managed to build on the side of the garage.

They weren't rich, Gus knew that, even though he'd never thought of their family as being poor. Gus's dad had worked for a car service in town before going to work for Uber. By now Gus realized that his father's main goal was to make sure that he and Angela never wanted for anything important. So Gus would never have asked for the basket that now extended from the outside wall of the garage, and the game court he had laid down—with a free-throw line and a lane and a three-point line.

This wasn't only Gus's practice court, it was Angela's, too. Gus just used it more. And he thought of it more as a birthday gift to him than to his sister. It wasn't a half court, really, more of a third of a court. But it was plenty big enough for a good game of two-on-two pickup, or even three-on-three.

When Gus had first seen it, he'd said, "Dad, this is too expensive."

"I work hard," his dad had said, "so I can invest in my children."

"I thought that meant our education."

"And your dreams. I've gotten to live out my dreams in America. Now I want you and your sister to live out yours."

"Even if they're just hoop dreams?"

"Even then."

The weather had gotten much colder over the past few days. If last Sunday had still felt like summer, today felt like the first day of winter to Gus. The sun had been out when his parents had driven him to the gym. But now Saturday had turned this dark shade of gray. Angela had said that there was even a possibility of snow in the forecast.

MIKE LUPICA

But right now Gus didn't care how cold it was. He just needed to be out here, pounding the ball, shooting it, chasing it down, shooting it again, working up a brand-new sweat. Or maybe he needed to just blow off some steam.

"Didn't you just finish playing basketball?" his mom had said when she saw him with his ball.

"I need to work," he'd said.

But once he was out here, he knew better. He loved the feel of the ball in his hands. He loved the way it felt when he'd release a shot and would just know it was going in from the way it felt coming off the fingers of his left hand. Playing basketball was never going to be like work to Gus, the way homework was, or chores.

Still, there was no getting around the fact that even with the day getting colder the longer he stayed out here, he was still hot about the way the game had ended.

It just made him throw himself even harder into what he was doing, as if only basketball could get him out of his funk. So he worked out on his right hand for a while. One of his personal goals before this season was over was to be as confident driving to his right as he was to his left. If guys continued to overplay him when he started to dribble left, Gus was going to make them pay by being able to cross over on them.

He would watch Steph Curry—and he watched Steph

Curry, live and on the Internet, as often as he could. Curry was his guy now, Curry was the reason he'd switched to number 30 this season. Gus tried to imagine what it must be like to be that kind of magician with the ball. His dad liked to say that watching Steph and what he could do with the ball, shooting it or passing it, was like watching some great artist with a brush in his hand. Or a great musician.

He drove to the basket now and made one of those one-hand, underhand scoop shots like Steph could make in his sleep, the ball kissing off the very top of the board.

He tried it with his right hand now, but missed. So he ran down the ball and tried it again, making it this time. Then he went over to the left corner and made the shot he was sure he could have made if Cassie had passed him the ball the way she should have.

He stopped now, breathing hard, because as much distance as he was trying to put between himself and the game, he couldn't get away from it. Or from Cassie.

Was he being too tough on her?

He stood at the free-throw line, ball on his hip, and asked himself another question:

If one game had been this tough, could their friendship survive a whole season?

Gus knew enough about himself, and how much he valued

friendship, to understand that this was the most important question of all, more important than any one about basketball.

He went back to basketball with a vengeance, working only on his outside shot now, playing a personal game of Around the World, starting in one corner and then working his way around the perimeter the way they did in the three-point shooting competition at the NBA's All-Star Saturday Night.

Then he went back again to the left corner, where he'd been standing when Cassie had driven for the basket, and stayed there until he made five in a row.

Then he missed two in a row.

Would I have missed today if she'd given me the chance to shoot?

He didn't know. Neither did she. Maybe neither one of them would know until a situation like it came up again, and she passed him the ball.

For now, it had taken just one game for Gus's fears about Cassie and the team and the season to be realized. Today the point guard *had* been out to prove a point.

Even if it meant losing by a point in the process.

ELEVEN

When he finished, he decided to ride his bike into town. Alone.

On a normal day, he would have been on his way to hang with Jack and Teddy and Cassie. But this wasn't a normal day.

When he told his mom what he was doing, she told him not to be long; it was starting to get dark earlier and earlier.

"Mom," he said, "I'm not a little kid."

"Ha!" she said, her voice as big as ever. "You know when you'll stop being my little boy? *Never* is when!"

Then she told him she loved him. Sometimes Gus thought that if she didn't tell him that about ten times a day, she'd give herself some sort of detention.

It was only three o'clock. But it was getting dark fast. Or maybe the color of the sky matched Gus's mood. As much as he kept telling himself that it was just one game, that it was only the first game of the season, he felt as badly as he did after they'd lost the football championship, even though he knew that made no sense.

The Christmas shopping season in downtown Walton had started, that was for sure. There was even Christmas music being piped in on the speakers set up along Main Street. Gus parked his bike in a rack in front of the new frozen yogurt store and locked it. He had some money with him and thought he might buy a smoothie after he had walked around a little bit.

He stopped in Bob's Sports and checked out a pair of Under Armour sneakers that he was going to put on his Christmas list. Steph was an Under Armour guy.

From there he went over to Walton Books and walked around in there. Gus really did love good books, and reading, especially novels about sports for guys his age.

It was funny, he thought. Books were the things he loved

talking about the most with Cassie Bennett. Oh, he'd talk about sports with her, and music, and movies, and videos, and even video games. But he talked about books with her more than he ever did with Jack or Teddy.

Books were their thing.

Just not today.

Gus stayed in the middle-grade section for a long time, looking at the covers of books he'd already read. It made him feel happier than he had since the game ended, being surrounded by stories he knew came out the way he wanted them to.

It wasn't until he walked out of the bookstore that a bad day got a little worse. Because if he hadn't looked up at the last second, he would have bumped right into Steve Kerrigan.

"Hey, Gustavo, watch where you're going!" Steve said, as if he wanted to be heard above the Christmas music. "You've had your head down since we lost the game. You gotta let go, dude."

Steve was with Brian McAuley, his best friend at school and on the team. Gus really liked Brian but had always thought he'd like him even more if he could figure out what he saw in Steve.

"Nah, I'm good," Gus said. "Just about to head home."

"Seriously, dude? You can't let this whole deal with Cassie get under your skin so much." Steve poked Brian with a playful elbow now and nodded at Gus. "Is he getting worked up because I'm talking about his girl? Or is he one of those hot-tempered types?"

Gus knew what he meant. You couldn't have the heritage he had without knowing that he meant a hot-tempered *Latin*. But he didn't want to get into an argument with Steve any more than he'd wanted to get into one with Cassie.

"I've told you before," Gus said, trying to keep himself calm and not *get* hot-tempered. "She's not my girl. She's never been my girl. She's my friend."

"Didn't look that way to me after the game," Steve said.

He was clearly enjoying himself, poking at Gus this way. But Gus wasn't. He forced himself to smile. "This may come as a shocker to you," he said. "But you don't always know everything about everything."

"See," Steve said, "now you're starting to do that hot-tempered thing all over again." He put out his hands. "Hey, don't blame me for losing the game."

There would be a day, Gus knew, when he wouldn't let Steve get away with his little digs about Gus being Dominican, as if Gus really was the outsider even though he'd grown up here the same as Steve Kerrigan had. But for now, he just wanted to go home. He thought of something Teddy had said once to a kid who was bothering him:

If he stayed around any longer, it might start to look like he was the jerk.

"See you at school," Gus said, and headed back down Main Street in the direction of the yogurt store.

"I wasn't trying to mess with you, Gustavo," Steve called out after him.

Gus didn't turn around, just waved his arm over his head and kept walking. *Perfect ending,* he thought, *to a perfect day, getting darker by the minute.*

Gus Morales felt as if he'd played a whole season already, and it had only started at eleven this morning.

TWELVE

If you didn't know that things had changed between Gus and Cassie, you might not have been able to pick up on that from watching them when they were together at school, in class or the hallway or at their lockers or in the cafeteria at lunch.

But Gus knew. So did Cassie, and Jack and Teddy.

It wasn't as if things had always been so easy for them. They had all helped Jack get through the loss of his brother, Brad. They had helped Teddy stop being the out-of-shape kid the other kids called Teddy Bear, and helped him during the football season when his father had come back into his life, and nearly helped turn him into a three-sport guy.

But when they were together, at least up until now, things *were* easy among the four of them, even when one of them—usually Gus—would get into it with Cassie over something or other that had set her hair on fire.

And somehow, in the end, they'd find a way to laugh everything off.

Just not now, especially not with the Warriors.

At Monday's practice, Gus could see Cassie trying harder than ever to fit in, trying to make sure everybody knew she was being unselfish, probably overpassing because she hadn't passed at the end of the Norris game, even passing on what could have been a layup and throwing the ball back out to Gus, who made a three.

But even then, and no matter what else was happening when Coach Keith would mix up the first and second units and they'd scrimmage against each other, Gus still couldn't shake the idea that when you looked at the Warriors, what you saw was Cassie and then everybody else.

The one girl out there with all the boys.

Gus's mom talked sometimes about the "elephant in the room," which she said was the thing everybody else in the room was thinking about even if they weren't talking about it. For Gus, Cassie was the elephant in the room. Or the gym.

In addition to that, Angela Morales was saying after both she and Gus had gotten home from practice on Monday night, things had also gotten sideways with Cassie's friends on the girls' team after all.

They were in Gus's room. The girls' team had practiced at Walton Middle tonight and the Warriors had gotten to practice at the high school.

"I thought you said you didn't care if Cassie bailed out on your team so she could come play on ours," Gus said.

"I didn't," Angela said. "And I don't."

Somehow she was stretched out on his bed, and Gus had ended up in the beanbag chair she'd given him last Christmas. He wasn't even sure how she'd gotten the bed before he did. But she had, because about this there was no question:

She acted like his older sister, even if she was just four minutes older.

Without a doubt, Angela was the boss of him.

"I didn't say I was the one who'd gotten all weirded out because she's playing with you guys and not us."

Gus said, "So it's some of your teammates who are chafed?"

"Totally," his sister said. "Mostly Katie and Gracie."

The girls had lost their first game on Sunday afternoon, to Hollis Hills, the first time most of the girls on the team had lost a game since they were in the sixth grade. Angela had replaced Cassie at point guard and had played decently enough. But she wasn't Cassie. Hollis Hills finally broke open what had been a close game and won by ten points.

"I thought Cassie's girlfriends were going to be happy for her," Gus said.

"I kind of thought they would be," Angela said. "But they're not. Katie and Cassie are barely speaking."

Welcome to the club, Gus thought.

"What's the problem? They think Cassie's on some kind of massive ego trip?" Gus said.

Angela gave him one of her full-throated laughs. "You mean as opposed to her normal ego trip?" she said. "Nah, but she just acts as if we're all supposed to be as wrapped up in what's happening to her as she is."

"I told you this was going to happen."

"No," Angela said. "You *thought* it might happen."

"They basically think she's telling them she's better than they are," Gus said. "Yeah, what could ever go wrong with that?"

Angela raised her eyebrows. "Well, there's a reason for that, brother. Cassie *is* way better than we are."

"Right," Gus said. "She's so good that her old team is 0–1

MIKE LUPICA

and her new team is 0–1 and she's got players on both teams mad at her."

"Only one player on her new team," his sister said. "You."

"You don't know that."

"Then tell me who else has their basketball shorts all tied up in knots besides my baby brother."

"I am not your little brother. I am your *twin* brother."

"You just act like a baby sometimes," she said. "I actually think you're happy that Katie and Gracie are mad at Cassie."

"Am not."

"Like now you get more members in the hating-on-Cassie club."

"I am not hating on her!"

Angela laughed again. "You really are too easy sometimes."

"Do you make fun of Katie and Gracie, too?"

"No," Angela said. "I tell them what I tell you: get over it already."

"You think this is all a big joke, don't you?"

"Actually, I don't," she said. "What I really think is that we're all good friends here, and we need to start acting that way. All of a sudden everybody in our grade is acting like some dopey episode of *Gossip Girls*. Including the boys."

"I didn't do anything," Gus said. "She did."

"It doesn't mean you can't do something about it."

Gus sank down lower into the beanbag chair, put his head back, closed his eyes, and made a sound that was part anger, part frustration.

"I just want to play basketball!" he said.

"Your first job is to be Cassie's friend," his sister said. "Stop thinking about this as if she's done something to you personally by making the Warriors. Think of her as a friend who needs your help. Ask yourself what you'd do if Jack or Teddy needed your help."

Gus stood up and started to walk out of the room, before he reminded himself that this was his room, not hers.

"Are you sure you're not a lot older than me than just a few minutes?" he said to her.

"Mom's right. I'm a very old soul."

"Can you read minds, too?"

"Occasionally."

"So you can read my mind right this minute and know I want my room back?"

She hopped off the bed, making it look easy. Angela didn't make a big deal of it, but she made a lot of things look easy, starting with being his sister.

"At least think about what I said," she said in his doorway. "You know Daddy's advice to you every time you have a problem with some other boy."

"He always tells me to be the bigger man," Gus said. "But usually that's just because he doesn't want me to get into a fight."

"Well, be the bigger man now," Angela said, "before this turns into a real fight between you and Cassie."

He did think about what she'd said, all night and all day at school. There was no basketball practice on Tuesday, so Gus decided that when he got off the bus, he would ride his bike over to Cassie's house and tell her he was going to have a whole new attitude from now on.

It was exactly what he started to do. But when he got to her corner, he stopped and looked down to the street where Cassie's driveway basket was, where she was laughing and playing one-on-one with Steve Kerrigan.

They couldn't see him. But he could see them, could see Cassie laughing and throwing Steve one sweet behind-the-back pass after another, a move he didn't even know she had. Gus watched them for a few minutes, and then turned his bike around and went back home.

THIRTEEN

Jack and Teddy didn't call Steve "Mayor Kerrigan" the way Gus sometimes did.

They had started calling him "the Goat."

G.O.A.T.

It stood for "Greatest of All Time." But they only meant it sarcastically.

"It's the way he thinks of himself," Teddy had explained to Gus.

"But isn't that the opposite of what 'goat' is supposed to mean in sports?" Gus asked. "Isn't the goat the guy who makes a turnover or an error and costs you the game?"

"Stuff changes," Jack said. "It's the way 'bad' can mean 'good.' Like when Mark Jackson is doing the game on ESPN and somebody is playing good and he says the guy is a very bad man."

"So you're telling me 'goat' is a good thing?"

"Nah," Teddy said. "It's just a way to make fun of him. Because a Goat like Steve thinks there can be only one greatest of all time: him."

"But let me ask you two deep thinkers a question," Gus said. "Doesn't Cassie think of herself the exact same way?"

Teddy looked at Jack. "Gus does make a good point."

"Maybe it all makes perfect sense," Gus said, "and explains why Cassie and Mayor Kerrigan, or the Goat, or whatever Steve is, are such close friends all of a sudden."

"You don't know that what kind of friends they are," Jack said, "just because you spied on them."

Gus corrected him. "Observed."

"Playing ball in her driveway one time?" Jack said.

"Dude," Teddy said, "you gotta stop letting every little thing Cassie does get to you. You're gonna make yourself nuts."

"More nuts," Jack said.

"Thanks loads," Gus said.

They were having lunch in the school cafeteria. Normally Cassie would have been with them, but she was getting some extra work in with her math teacher. Teddy said that really should have been the big news of the day at Walton Middle School, Cassie admitting she needed help in any subject. Or any*thing*.

"By the way?" Gus said. "Maybe it's not such a little thing, because if Cassie really wants to hang around with that jerk, what's that say about somebody who's supposed to be as smart as she is?"

Jack grinned. "Except in math."

"Well, today in math," Teddy said.

"You guys still think this is funny."

"Little bit," Teddy said.

"Whose side are you both on?" Gus said.

Jack Callahan wasn't grinning when he said, "I'm on everybody's side."

He paused and added, "The way all four of us are supposed to be."

Both Jack and Teddy had made it clear that even though things weren't getting any better between Gus and Cassie, they didn't want to take sides. More than any of them, Gus knew, Jack hated any kind of tension: with his friends, with his teammates, even here at school. He genuinely wanted everybody to get along. He'd been that way from the first time he and Gus had met, back in first grade. Gus had seen him become even more that way after Jack's older brother Brad had died in a dirt-bike accident. Now more than ever, Jack Callahan refused to sweat the small stuff.

"Maybe," Teddy said, "Steve is the one wanting to hang out with Cassie because he knows it will get under the skin of his dear friend Gustavo." He made sure to put air quotes around "Gustavo" so Gus would know he was joking.

"And if he does get under your skin, he really does get to feel like the greatest of all time," Jack said.

"Well, I'm glad you guys have figured everything out," Gus said.

"You could probably figure things out if you and Cassie would just talk the way you used to," Teddy said.

"Yeah," Gus said, "because the two of us talking has worked out great so far, don't you think?"

"Here's what I really think," Jack said. "Everything is gonna get a lot easier once we get a win."

Gus shook his head as he stared at his best friend in the world. "Man, I wish I had your attitude."

"Everybody does," Teddy said.

The Warriors had just one more game before they took a break for Christmas. It was against the Moran Mustangs, always one of their biggest rivals because Moran was just ten minutes away from Walton.

The Mustangs' best player was a kid named Amir El-Amin, who played small forward the same as Gus did. They'd been guarding each other since the sixth grade, and Gus figured nothing was going to change. They were pretty much the same size, they both were good outside shooters, they both loved competing against each other. They loved competing, period. Neither one of them was a trash-talker. It was just Gus's best against Amir's, and they'd see who was better today.

Amir was also a stellar defensive back in football and would have guarded Gus there, but he'd sprained his ankle the week before the Walton-Moran game. And because he didn't play baseball, Gus hadn't seen him since the last basketball season.

Gus knew that both of Amir's parents were doctors, because a couple of years ago, when Angela had partially torn a ligament in her knee playing soccer, she'd ended up being treated by Amir's dad.

The game was in the gym at Moran Middle School. During warm-ups Gus had jogged down to say hello to Amir. It was part of the fun of growing up with guys in the same league: after a while you felt you had some history with them. The last time they'd met up on a basketball court, the history had been on Walton's side, because Jack had made a steal right before the

MIKE LUPICA

buzzer and fed Gus for the basket that had won them the game.

"Go easy on us today," Amir said. "I've been replaying last year's game *all* year."

"Whoa," Gus said. "*You* go easy on *me.* I seem to recall you dropped twenty on me in that game."

Amir shrugged and grinned, then leaned in close to Gus, practically whispering to him. "A girl on the team? Seriously?"

Gus turned and looked down the court just as Steve Kerrigan fed Cassie the ball in the left-hand corner, and she made a high-arcing shot.

"She's good," Gus said.

No matter what was going on with him and Cassie, Gus was never going to say anything bad about her to an opposing player, even one he respected.

"What's it been like?" Amir said.

That got a smile out of Gus. "It's been a little different."

"Yo," Amir said. "Am I allowed to get after it when she's got the ball?"

"Just giving you a heads-up," Gus said, "but you should probably be more worried about her getting after *you.*"

Coach went with the same starting five he'd used against Norris and didn't make his first subs until there were two minutes left in the first quarter. Then he put Cassie in for Brian McAuley and gave Steve Kerrigan a breather too, replacing him with Len Ritchie. The game was tied at that point, and was still tied at the end of the quarter.

Coach put Steve back in and left Cassie out there. And over the next few minutes it was clear to Gus that Steve had become Cassie's go-to guy. It didn't mean she was ignoring Jack and Gus, who'd been doing most of the scoring so far for the Warriors. But once they were into a play, she was looking to get the ball to Steve the first chance she got, even though Steve's shot had been off so far.

But he was still her first option. The Warriors tried to keep up with the Mustangs, and particularly with Amir, who was smoking hot from the outside no matter how closely Gus was guarding him.

Over the last two minutes of the half, Amir made two three-pointers, both times with Gus's hand in his face, and would have had another three-pointer if his foot hadn't been scraping the line. With Gus and Jack and Steve each missing shots at the other end, Amir's eight points were the difference in the game, putting the Mustangs ahead, 30–23.

As Gus walked toward the Warriors bench, Steve Kerrigan fell in beside him.

"You're gonna need to do a better job guarding your friend Abdul in the second half," Steve said.

Gus stopped and looked at him. "I've been working my

butt off," he said. "And for your information, his name is Amir."

"Abdul, Amir, whatever," Steve said. "We need to find a way for him to stop bombing away."

"Is that your idea of a joke?" Gus said. "Calling him a bomber because of his name?"

Steve tried to look innocent. "Hey, I didn't say that. You did."

"Right," Gus said. "I just imagined the whole thing." Steve started to walk away, but Gus put a hand on his arm. Steve stared at Gus's hand. But Gus didn't remove it right away.

"And do yourself a favor," Gus said to him. "Don't let anybody else hear you making fun of Amir's name. Starting with Amir."

Steve shook his head. "Man, it's like my dad says. You can't say anything these days without offending somebody."

Gus watched him walk away, thinking, *Only if they're dumb enough to look at the world the way you do.*

Goat.

Gus's dad had been a good baseball player when he was young, just not good enough to get the kind of professional contract that some of his friends would get.

But he was as smart about sports as any coach Gus had ever had, and sometimes had a lot more common sense than most of the commentators they would listen to on television.

One of the things he always told Gus about the game he was playing was this:

Control the things you can control.

He could control doing a better job on Amir in the second half, even if the guy had been making crazy shots at the end of the first. And he could control knocking down his own shots when he got them, something he started to do about halfway through the third quarter. Gus didn't know why he was feeling it all of a sudden. But he was. So was Jack Callahan. Maybe it was because Cassie was on the bench and not looking to throw the ball to Steve the first time he called for it. But for these few minutes, the Warriors were finally clicking on offense.

Brian kept doing his job as point guard and feeding either Gus or Jack every chance he got, at least when Gus and Jack weren't feeding each other, and feeding *off* each other at the same time Gus was finally putting the clamps on Amir at the other end of the court.

Brian and Steve Kerrigan might have been best friends off the court, but on the court, Brian was doing what good point guards were supposed to do: feeding the Warriors' hot hands, Gus and Jack. It was if the two of them had turned into Steph Curry and Klay Thompson of the real Warriors, the Splash Brothers. By the time the third-quarter buzzer sounded, that eight-point halftime deficit for the Warriors had become an eight-point lead. Coach had subbed around Gus and Jack, getting Wayne Coffey into the game and Jake and Len Ritchie and Henry Koepp. But he had left Gus and Jack out there for the whole quarter, not taking them out until the start of the fourth.

The five on the court to start the quarter for the Warriors were Cassie, Steve, Henry, Wayne, and Jake. But after everything had been falling for the Warriors at the start of the second half, now nothing was. And Amir had gotten his stroke back. With five minutes left, and the game tied at 48, Coach put his starting five back on the court, even though Brian had three fouls.

A minute and a half later, Brian was called for an offensive foul, then a reach-in foul on Amir at the other end. He had fouled out that quickly, and Cassie was back in the game.

Another close game for her, Gus thought. *Another close game for all of us.* And they all had the same job the rest of the way, which meant finding a way to make this Saturday end better than last Saturday had.

"We are not losing," Gus said to Jack.

"Who said anything about losing?" Jack said.

Gus immediately stole the ball from Amir, drove the length of the court, and got his first easy basket of the game. But the Mustangs came right back. The Mustangs' center cleared Gus out on a screen, and Steve was slow switching over on Amir. Amir made another three-pointer. The Mustangs were back ahead by one.

Jack hit a jumper, putting the Warriors up one, then blocked a shot by the kid he was guarding, Cory Allen, and threw the ball up ahead to Gus, who pulled up and hit a jumper from just inside the three-point line.

The Warriors were ahead by three.

A minute and ten seconds left.

Gus smothered Amir at the other end. Amir gave the ball up to his center, Donnie Falco, who up-faked Steve, drew contact as Steve was on the way down, and banked home a layup.

Steve had gone for Donnie's fake because he was trying to make another flashy blocked shot, having gotten a couple of Donnie's shots already. He ended up giving up a three-point play instead when Donnie made his free throw. The game was tied. Coach Keith called time-out.

As the Warriors walked off the court, Gus heard Steve say to Cassie, "Guy traveled before the shot."

As usual Steve had been doing a lot of talking all game long, picking his spots, keeping his voice low, trying to get under Donnie's skin, or Amir's, or at least make them lose their focus. It just hadn't been working today.

And when Amir heard what Steve said to Cassie as he was

walking past them, he couldn't help himself, and laughed.

Steve wheeled on him. "You think something's funny, Amin?"

"*El*-Amin," Amir said.

"Does it really make a difference?" Steve said.

Even now he was trying to get a rise out of Amir. But Amir wouldn't play along. He just smiled and said, "Play the game."

In the huddle, Coach told them to spread the court and then run a play that had been working all day: Gus and Jack out on the wings, and then crisscrossing like a couple of wide receivers in football, hoping one of the guys guarding them would get picked off. Or both.

But as soon as they did, they all heard Steve Kerrigan yell, "Cassie!" and wave his arm for the ball, even though Gus had completely lost Amir and was wide open on the left wing.

Cassie never looked at Gus. She lobbed the ball over Donnie Falco to Steve. As soon as she did, Amir dropped down to help out, putting himself between Steve and the basket.

With Amir and Donnie double-teaming Steve Kerrigan, Gus couldn't have been more open if everybody on the Mustang team had gone home.

But it didn't matter. Maybe Steve was unhappy that Gus and Jack had been carrying the offense. Maybe he saw his chance to show up Amir.

But as he moved into the lane, Amir moved with him, hands straight up in the air. "Steve!" Gus yelled, but Steve ignored him, determined to make his move around Amir, even though there was no room, until he finally dribbled the ball off his foot and out of bounds.

It was the Mustangs' ball, with fifteen seconds left. Their coach didn't call a time-out, just stayed in his seat and smiled at his players and said, "Play."

Control what you can control, Gus told himself.

Amir got the ball at the free-throw line. Gus was as close to him as you could be without touching him as Amir went up in the air. He had made more than one shot today with Gus hanging all over him and looked to be trying another one, even though it was going to be a force.

Only he wasn't shooting.

He was passing to Donnie Falco. Steve Kerrigan was so sure Amir was shooting that he had turned his back, getting himself into rebounding position. Now Donnie was the one who was wide open. He was about ten feet from the basket when he took Amir's pass and made the soft floater that won the game for the Mustangs by a basket.

Just like that the Warriors were 0–2.

Amir was still next to Gus when Donnie's shot went through the basket, barely even causing a ripple in the net.

MIKE LUPICA

"That guy's not nearly as good as he thinks he is," Amir said, and they both knew he was talking about Steve.

Somehow Steve heard him. "You talking about me?" he said. "Say it to my face."

Amir was already walking away. "Game's over, dude."

"We'll see you again!" Steve yelled, before Jack stepped in front of him.

Amir was still with Gus.

"I knew he wasn't going to pass the ball at the other end," Amir said. "But why didn't your point guard pass it to you?"

Gus said that was a good question, and he was going to ask Cassie, first chance he got. He just wasn't going to do it here, in front of everybody. He was going to wait until they were back in Walton.

That talk everybody wanted him to have with Cassie?

He was ready to have it now.

FOURTEEN

He didn't tell Cassie he was on his way over. If she wasn't home, or if Steve Kerrigan was with her the way he had been the last time Gus had made this trip, he would just turn his bike around and head back.

The ride over gave him time to clear his head, or at least try to.

He knew it wasn't the end of the world that the season had started out with two losses. Maybe, he thought, it was just the law of averages catching up with him, after the tear his teams had been on lately; not just the law of averages for him, but for Jack and Teddy, and even Cassie, too. Starting with softball in the spring, she'd been in more winning games than anybody their age in Walton.

Maybe they were all due for some bad luck, or even a bad season, whether Cassie was playing for the Warriors or not.

But it didn't change the fact that they should have won at least one of the first two games. And could have won both of them. Coach Keith said that it was never just one play or one call that cost your team a game, even though people always focused on the last minute, or even the last play, and forgot everything that happened before that. Gus knew Coach was right. Still, if Cassie had just passed the ball to Gus instead of Steve today, and if she had passed to *anybody* at the end of the Norris game, they might be 2–0, and he might not be on his way over to Cassie's house.

But he was.

When he rounded the corner this time, she wasn't shooting around with Steve at the hoop in her driveway. Gus left his bike over by the garage, walked around to the front of the house, and rang the doorbell.

Cassie's mom answered.

"Gus!" she said. "What a nice surprise."

"Nice to see you, too, Mrs. Bennett. Is Cassie home?"

"She is," she said, and showed Gus into the house, calling upstairs as she did, telling Cassie that she had a visitor.

When Cassie appeared at the top of the stairs, Gus could see that she was the one getting a surprise, though her face told him she didn't share her mom's opinion that it was a nice one.

"Hey," she said.

"Hey," he said.

"Did I miss the text or call telling me you were coming over?" Cassie said.

Mrs. Bennett was still standing with Gus. "Cassie Bennett!" she said. "Is that any way to greet one of your best friends?"

"I forgot," she said, and Gus wasn't sure in that moment whether she meant she'd forgotten her manners, or forgotten that Gus was one of her best friends.

Mrs. Bennett walked away. Cassie was still leaning over the banister.

"You doing anything right now?" Gus said.

"I'm talking to you."

"Want to?"

"Want to what?"

"Talk to me."

Cassie shrugged, as if she had no choice in the matter now that he was here. "You want to come up?"

"Let's take a walk over to the dock."

"It's cold out."

"Wuss," he said, talking to her the way he used to talk to her before this basketball season had begun. Gus thought he might have detected a quick smile, but maybe just because he wanted to.

"Let me get a sweatshirt," she said. When she came back from her room, she was wearing the green Packers hoodie Jack had gotten her last Christmas. Aaron Rodgers, the Packers quarterback, was Jack's favorite player and had become Cassie's, too.

The dock Gus referred to was the one that extended into the pond behind houses in Cassie's neighborhood. In the summer, it was one of their favorite places to be, whether they were standing at the end of it skipping rocks, or putting Jack's canoe into the water, or just lying on their backs and taking in some sun. When they had no other place they had to be, this dock was the place they most wanted to be, basically.

Gus was hoping that if they could sit there, just the two of them, they could find their way back to where they used to be.

That was the plan, anyway.

It *was* cold when they got to the dock. But the wind had died down, and the sun was back out from behind the clouds. So even though it was a long way from feeling like a summer day, it didn't feel like winter, either.

Gus and Cassie sat facing each other. Cassie had her arms wrapped around her knees. She had hardly said anything on the way over, as quiet as she could be, even on a five-minute walk. Teddy had always said that the only thing that really scared Cassie Bennett was having an unspoken thought.

"This stinks," Gus said, finally.

"Losing always stinks."

Gus smiled; he couldn't help himself. "You don't know anything about losing," he said. "It hardly ever happens to you."

"Maybe that's why I feel the way I do after I do lose," she said. "It's not something I want to get used to."

"I've noticed," Gus said.

"So what stinks, other than losing?"

She wasn't going to make this easy.

"You and me," he said. "It's just the two of us who are messed up. It's messing up the team." He paused and said, "And now it's costing us games."

"You're saying that I'm the reason we're losing?" she said.

"That's not what I said, and it's not what I mean."

"Then what do you mean?" Cassie said.

Gus waited, wanting to get this exactly right, not sure when he'd get another chance to do that if this was one more thing that got messed up.

He said, "Sometimes I just think you're worrying about stuff that has nothing to do with us winning the game."

Her eyes got bright now, like they did when she was fired up about something, like they were on fire all of a sudden.

"I don't want to win?" she said.

"Didn't say that, either."

"Then say what you mean."

"I'm trying to."

"Since you suddenly seem to know everything about how to win basketball games, give me some examples."

He took a deep breath. "I just thought that maybe you should have passed the ball to me at the end. Or to Jack."

"But not Steve, right? Because even though he's as good a scorer as we have, you think he's a jerk."

"No," Gus said. "Well, yeah, I do think he's a jerk. But he wasn't one of our best scorers today, and Jack and I had been knocking down open shots the whole game."

"Let me ask you something," Cassie said. "Are we going to do this all season? Am I going to hear about it every time I don't make the play you want me to make?"

Gus looked past her, to the water. But there was no help for him out there. "No," he said. "I'm not your coach."

"No kidding."

From the time the game had ended, he'd thought Cassie had made the wrong play. He was sure he was right about that. But then how come he couldn't find the right words to tell her that, *without* sounding like he was her coach?

"What do you want me to do," Cassie said, "other than go back to the girls' team?"

Gus shook his head quickly from side to side, hoping that would clear it.

No chance.

"Why are you being like this?" was the best he could do.

"Why are *you* being like this?" Cassie said, her voice rising.

"I just want us to be on the same page."

"We're not even in the same book," Cassie said.

"So why do you think I came over?"

"To make me feel worse about us losing than I already do."

"You really think that?"

She nodded, her eyes locked on his as she did. "Yeah," she said. "I do." She kept nodding. "I still think you're mad because I made the team. And I think you're mad that I don't think Steve is the worst person in the world."

"I don't like the guy," he said. "But I can play on the same team with him."

"So let me get this straight," Cassie said. "Somebody you don't like, *him* you're okay with. But somebody who's one of your best friends, or at least is supposed to still be one of your best friends, you can't figure it out."

Gus could see how angry she was, or maybe how hurt. Somehow by coming over here, he'd made things worse. And they seemed to be getting worse by the second.

"Sometimes I feel like I don't even know you," he said, knowing how lame that sounded.

"What you don't really know," Cassie said, "is what it's like being me."

"You didn't have to do this."

Now Cassie didn't look angry, just sad. "You mean try out for this team?" she said. "If you ever did know me, you'd know I did have to do it."

She stood up.

"We're done here," she said.

She didn't walk away from him, because she knew his bike was back at her house. She waited for him to get up, and then the two of them walked back to her house together, but more apart than they'd ever been.

FIFTEEN

It was a good Christmas in the Morales family.

Gus got the big gift he'd been hoping for, a pair of Steph Curry Under Armour sneakers. His dad then ordered him to use his new kicks to kick-start the Warriors' season after their Christmas break.

Angela, who loved photography, got the new small Polaroid camera, one that wasn't much bigger than an iPhone but could print out black-and-white pictures as soon as she took them.

There were never a lot of presents under their tree. But that had never mattered to the twins. They were always thrilled to receive the gifts they did, big and small, because they knew how hard their parents worked to buy them. These days their dad seemed to be working more and more hours than ever. Their mom had gone back to working a few days a week as a house-keeper, so that was a bit of a change for Gus and Angela, not always having her there when they came home from school or an early practice.

Gus had bought his mom a sketchbook, and paint, and paintbrushes, because she had also gone back to painting in her spare time. He and Angela had chipped in and bought their dad a new baseball glove, since he had gone back to play-ing in a softball league the previous summer with a lot of his Dominican friends, despite complaining the whole time that his knees now felt older than the Walton River. He immedi-ately found some oil and rubbed some into the pocket, just the way Gus did when he got a new mitt, and stuck in an old ball, tied a string around the glove and ball, and put it under a couch cushion.

"Does that really help break in a mitt?" Gus said.

"If it doesn't," his dad said, smiling, "then I have wasted a lot of time in my life sitting on a lot of mitts."

By Christmas afternoon Jack and his parents had gone over

to Hollis Hills to have dinner with his mom's sister and her family. Teddy was still at home, though. His dad had come over for an early lunch, because even though his parents had divorced a long time ago, they were getting along better now than they ever had. But as soon as lunch was over, Teddy's dad was on his way to the airport. He worked for ESPN and had to fly out to California for one of their big bowl games.

Teddy called Gus and told him to get over to his house right now to play with the new Xbox One unit his dad had given him. He'd also gotten a new mitt, a catcher's mitt—for next season—and even a drone.

"He wanted to spoil me a little, since this is his first Christmas back in Walton," Teddy said. "And I thought it would have been just plain cruel of me not to let him."

Gus laughed. Teddy Madden made him laugh more than anybody he knew. "You did the right thing," he said.

"It wasn't just about me," Teddy said. "If I'd turned down Xbox One, think of all the people who would have been hurt."

"You really should get some kind of trophy for doing this," Gus said.

"Come on over," Teddy said. "We'll play NBA and then just veg."

Even though Teddy continued to be in the best shape of his life, he could still veg with the best of them.

So they played NBA 2K17 until Teddy said he was starting to lose feeling in his fingers. It was almost time for the Warriors to play the Spurs in the big television game on TV, a game Gus had been looking forward to all week. As much as he loved Steph, he also loved team basketball enough to appreciate that the Spurs played as beautiful and unselfish a game as he'd ever seen.

At the end of the first quarter, Teddy turned to Gus and said, "I've decided that I like watching basketball more than I like playing it."

"You would have helped our team and you know it. I'm betting that you were the last guy cut."

Teddy grinned and made a motion like he was sweeping sweat off his forehead.

"Whew!" he said. "If you're right, that was a close one!"

Then he turned to Gus and said, "Hey, I've got an idea. Why don't we invite Cassie over to watch the second half?"

"You're doing it again," Gus said.

"Doing what?" Teddy said, trying to look innocent.

"Trying to be what my mother keeps joking that Cassie and I need."

"What's that?"

"A couples counselor!"

"Am not."

"Are too."

"You're telling me you don't want me to invite her over?"

"You want the truth? No."

"C'mon," Teddy said. "It's Christmastime. Nobody fights on Christmas, except maybe the Warriors and the Spurs. It would be good for you two to just chill."

"Trust me," Gus said, "things are way chill enough between us."

"You guys haven't talked?"

"Not since school let out."

"Hey, look on the bright side!" Teddy said. "If you're not talking, at least you're not fighting."

"Is that all you got?"

"Pretty much."

Gus let out a sigh so loud the force of it actually surprised him.

"Things have to get better, right?" he said to Teddy.

"Sitting where I'm sitting?" Teddy said. "They can't get any worse."

"You know what we could use?" Gus said. "A nice blowout win next Saturday."

The Warriors didn't get one. They got another close game instead.

And this time Cassie passed Gus the ball at the end.

SIXTEEN

The game was against the Rawson Raptors, in the gym at Walton Middle School, the Saturday before school started up again.

The Raptors had won their first two games and were led by Chris Charles, the quarterback on the Rawson football team. He was tall and left-handed and played center for them. Only he didn't play like a center. He played like somebody who could be playing any of the five positions on the court, including point guard if the Raptors had needed him to. It was because of his outside shooting, and his ability to handle the ball. Sometimes he did set up in the low blocks, the way most centers did. But he was just as likely to bring the ball up, or step beyond the three-point line and fire away. Gus remembered all the elements of his game from last season, knowing that there were times when Chris would grab a defensive rebound, lead the fast break himself, and finish with either a layup or a jumper.

He hadn't lost much from one season to the next, because he had been dominating Steve Kerrigan for most of the game, something most centers in their league couldn't come close to doing. Chris was getting his shots where he wanted them and when he wanted them, and rebounding like a champ at both ends of the court.

On top of all that, he was getting to Steve. He didn't do it by chirping at him, or doing anything to show him up. He was doing it by being the better player today, by a lot.

In a Warriors huddle a couple of minutes into the fourth quarter, Steve said, "The refs are still letting that guy get away with murder."

They all knew who he was talking about. Nobody else on the Warriors agreed with him, or even responded. They'd all been watching the same game, which meant watching Chris do pretty much whatever he wanted against Steve Kerrigan.

MIKE LUPICA

But even with that, the game was tied. Coach Keith had finally gone to a box-and-one defense against Chris at the start of the quarter, to slow him down or at least give him a second look, or both. Len Ritchie came off the bench to guard Chris, or at least try to guard him. The other four guys on the court for the Warriors basically played a two-two zone and tried to surround Chris every time he touched the ball, especially when he was close to the basket. Gus helped, Jack helped. Cassie helped. Gus thought they were bringing a whole new definition to the idea of "help defense." They all knew that Coach thought if you didn't teach man-to-man defense, you weren't teaching real basketball.

But what was more real right now was trying to win their first game of the season.

"Time to change the rules of engagement," he said when he told them they were going to the box-and-one.

The change worked. Chris was too unselfish not to pass the ball out of double teams, and sometimes triple teams. So he kept looking for open teammates. But those teammates were missing the shots he'd been making all game long. So Coach's defense was working, just because it was taking the ball out of Chris's hands.

It was 48–48 with six minutes left. By now Gus and Jack were doing most of the scoring. Cassie had been out there with them for most of the second half. Steve had just come back into the game, even though he had four fouls. They were going to make their stand right here. There was no time to worry about the close games they'd already lost. Gus and Cassie might not be best friends right now, but they were trying to be the best teammates they could. She was playing her smartest floor game and holding her own against the Raptors' point guard, Alex Trueba.

For the first time this season, Gus felt as if he and Jack and Cassie really were playing like a team. If she made a good pass, he told her. When he'd make another shot, she'd give him a fast low five on her way past him, as they were getting back on defense. Maybe, Gus thought, you didn't have to talk your way through stuff after all. Maybe you could play your way through. And maybe, just maybe, you could finally win the kind of game you'd been losing. Right after the Raptors went on a rip early in the fourth quarter, the Warriors came right back at them.

During their last time-out, Teddy came over to Gus, trusty score book in hand, and said, "You and Cass and Jack just keep doing what you're doing. We've outscored them 12–4 over the last four minutes."

"Got it, Assistant Coach Madden," Gus said.

"You know I'm right," Teddy said.

"Actually," Gus said, "I do."

MIKE LUPICA

It was clear by now that the only way Teddy could have been more into these games was if he were playing in them. In addition to keeping track of points and fouls and turnovers and time-outs, he always had a separate piece of paper next to him on the scoring table—he sat next to Coach Keith—on which he kept track of the kind of run the Warriors had been on. More and more, with Coach's encouragement, Teddy would lean over and share his real-time numbers while the game was going on.

So it was 56–56 with two minutes left, Warriors' ball. Steve was fighting Chris for position down low, waving for the ball as he did, even though Gus couldn't remember him scoring a single point since halftime.

Cassie threw him the ball.

Steve forced up the kind of shot that Chris had been refusing to force up, out of tight coverage, at the other end of the court. Chris not only blocked the shot; he also managed to hit it off Steve and out of bounds.

Raptors' ball. A minute and forty seconds left.

"I got fouled!" Steve yelled at Cassie, who was closest to him, as he got back on defense. Cassie ignored him and just ran to cover Alex Trueba, focusing on the next play.

Steve, though, was still fixed on the last one, even looking up to where his parents were sitting in the crowd, putting his arms out, as if what had just happened wasn't his fault. As soon as he turned his head, Chris Charles blew past him toward the basket, took a long feed from Alex, and made an easy layup.

It was 58–56.

Once Cassie was past half court with the ball, Gus set a screen for Jack. As soon as Jack had cleared his man, and Gus's, Cassie fed him perfectly. Jack released his shot, and Gus was already getting back on defense. Sometimes with Jack, you watched the finish, and you just knew. Gus knew. Nothing but net. Game tied again.

They were under a minute. The Raptors worked the ball around on the outside while Chris ran from one side of the court to the other, and even down the baseline, trying to get free from Len Ritchie. The second he did, Alex threw him the ball. Steve came over to help out.

"In front of him!" Coach yelled from the Warriors' bench.

But even now, even having had this bad a game, Steve Kerrigan couldn't get out of his own way. He did the opposite of what Coach wanted, and tried to reach around Chris from behind and make a steal. But Chris either saw him coming, or sensed that he was coming, with the sixth sense guys that good sometimes had. He spun the other way, losing both Len and Steve in the process, and suddenly found himself with a clear path to the basket.

MIKE LUPICA

But somehow, almost out of nowhere, Cassie was there, blocking his path.

Chris either didn't see her, his eyes fixed on the rim, or couldn't stop himself, and plowed right into her.

For a second Gus thought that the kid who had been the star of the game might get the whistle, and not the girl who had clearly established position.

But Cassie got the whistle, and the call. The ref closest to the play put his hand behind his head and patted it a couple of times, the signal for offensive foul.

So it was Warriors' ball, game tied, twenty seconds left. Gus looked over at their bench, and for one really bad moment thought Coach was about to signal to the ref closest to him for a time-out, even though Gus knew they were out of time-outs—Coach had just told them that a few minutes before. Gus was about to yell over to him, but Teddy beat him to it. He stood up at the scorer's table and yelled, "Coach!" himself, pointing to his score book and shaking his head, saving the Warriors from getting a technical foul at the worst possible moment; maybe saving the Warriors, period.

Coach reached back and gave Teddy a quick high five. Then he turned back to the court, and his players, and shouted one word:

"Play."

Alex Trueba reached in on Cassie as she brought the ball out of the backcourt and nearly stole the ball, even getting his hand on it and knocking it away. But Cassie was quicker to it and gained control, then headed for the top of the key.

Gus and Jack were on opposite wings. They looked at each other. Then Jack gave a quick nod, and sprinted across the court. This time he was setting the pick for Gus, who came around the screen, on his way to one of his sweet spots, the foul line extended on the left side. As he did, he could hear Steve Kerrigan yelling for the ball. Briefly Gus wondered if Cassie would give in to him, again.

Only she didn't. Gus's man hadn't switched, and Jack's man had stayed on him, so Gus was wide open. Cassie threw him the ball. When it was in his hands, he gave a quick look at the block above the backboard.

There were seven seconds left.

Gus Morales didn't hesitate. He took one dribble, squared his shoulders . . .

And promptly fired up an air ball.

MIKE LUPICA

SEVENTEEN

He was so sure the shot was going to fall that he just stood there and watched it instead of following it to the basket in case he missed.

He didn't crash the boards the way the rest of his teammates did. He didn't box out the Rawson player closest to him, because like Coach Keith taught, just put a body on *some*body.

As the last seconds of regulation ticked off the clock, Gus

was nothing more than a spectator. He just watched.

This was what he saw:

He saw Jake and Chris Charles fighting for the ball. He saw it tip off Chris's fingers and float toward Cassie. The clock showed four seconds now. Cassie must have seen it, because she didn't take time to catch the ball—she just batted it with both hands toward the basket like a volleyball player, over Chris Charles and into the hands of Steve Kerrigan, who caught the ball and shot it in the same motion, the ball softly hitting the backboard and then hitting the net even more softly one second before the horn sounded.

As soon as it did, Gus turned and looked at the ref to his right, who'd been watching the ball and the clock from outside the three-point line. He didn't hesitate as he signaled that it was a good basket, that Steve had gotten it off in time, and that the Warriors had beaten the Rawson Raptors.

Cassie ran over and launched herself into the air, as she and Steve did a flying shoulder bump. Gus was about to run over and congratulate both of them, but he never got the chance.

Cassie came straight for him.

"Did I finally make the right play?" she said. "Or should I have passed it back out to you?"

Gus realized that he still hadn't moved, that he was still

standing in the same spot from which he'd fired up his brick. He'd made his last three shots before it; he was sure his shot was going to win the game. And then he hadn't hit anything. Now he felt as if Cassie had hit him with a brick.

Even when they were finally winners, he still felt like a loser.

EIGHTEEN

Most days Gus and Cassie still sat with Jack and Teddy at lunch. They didn't ignore each other, they still talked to each other, about the Warriors and classes and whatever else was going on at school, now that second semester had started.

Gus just never felt as if they were talking *to* each other. They didn't fight the way they used to—what Jack used to call the Gus-Cassie Debates. And the weird part of what was going on between them, the way they were both so dug in about her playing on the Warriors, was that Gus found himself missing those fights. It was just another part of missing the way things used to be. Maybe things would get back to normal when basketball season was over.

Or maybe they wouldn't.

At least today at lunch, there was no awkwardness between them, maybe because the argument of the day didn't involve anybody at their end of the table. It was about who was going to be president of the ninth grade next year at Walton Middle School, Steve Kerrigan or Marianna Ruiz.

The way they did it at their school was this: They held the election in the spring, so that whoever was elected president could hit the ground running next September, and also have a full year on the job. And you only got one year. If you were president of the eighth grade, the way Katie Cummings was, you weren't allowed by the school charter to run again.

But their grade was already on fire at the prospect of Steve and Marianna running against each other. Their fathers had just run against each other for mayor in the fall. Their campaigns hadn't even started yet, and already kids in their grade were talking about Steve versus Marianna like they did about a big game in sports. Only they were treating it like it was going to be the biggest game of the second semester, in any sport.

"Do you think Marianna would have decided to run if Steve hadn't?" Teddy said.

"She told me during soccer that she was going to do it," Cassie said.

"Was that before or after her dad lost to Mr. Kerrigan?" Jack said.

Cassie frowned, thinking that one over. "You know, I can't remember. What I mostly remember is how mad she was that Mr. Kerrigan kept finding ways to make sure Walton wasn't run by outsiders."

She put air quotes around "outsiders."

"He meant people with names like Ruiz or Morales," Gus said. "I think if Marianna hadn't decided to run, my sister would have. She was as angry about Mr. Kerrigan as Marianna was."

Teddy said, "I think Mr. Kerrigan was just trying to sound like Donald Trump, when he was talking about building that big wall between the United States and Mexico."

"Maybe Mr. Kerrigan thinks that all people with last names like mine and Marianna's are the same," Gus said.

"Yeah," Jack said. "Different."

There was no question that Walton was a different town than it used to be. No one was exactly sure when it happened or why it happened. But the town was about 40 percent Hispanic now. Gus knew because his parents talked about it all the time, what they called the changing "face" of Walton. It was one of the reasons why Spanish was being taught now at Walton Middle. More and more, Gus would hear conversations in Spanish in the hall, at his locker, on the bus.

It was why more people had voted for mayor than at any other time in the history of the town. Angela Morales had not only followed it closely, she'd volunteered to help out at Michael Ruiz's headquarters on weekends. Angela kept telling Gus that the race was more than Steve's dad running against Marianna's dad. It was the old Walton versus the new one.

The old Walton won. Barely.

So everybody at Walton Middle, and not just the eighth graders, was totally geeked—a Teddy word—about the mayor's son and the losing candidate's daughter running against each other in a school election. There had even been a story written about it in the *Walton Dispatch*, and on Patch.com.

And because of all the interest, the teachers had decided to drag the campaign out, to the point where it was going to last a whole month and end right around the same time the basketball season did.

"You think this is going to put too much pressure on Steve," Teddy said, "basically trying to win two things at the same time?"

"Are you serious?" Gus said. "Not as long as people are talking about him."

"You know," Cassie said, "he's still our teammate."

Gus was about to say that Steve thought he was a basketball team all by himself, but Teddy jumped in ahead of him, like somebody cutting a line.

"We're just lucky to be in the same grade as someone as well-rounded as he is," Teddy said, grinning. "And if you don't believe that, just ask him."

"He's not as bad as you guys think," Cassie said.

"He couldn't be," Teddy said, and allowed himself to take a high five from Gus.

Jack was the one grinning now. "That's pretty much where we are with the Goat," he said.

They were halfway through the regular season. Over the past few weeks there had been a lot of winning, and hardly any drama. The Warriors had won five in a row and lost none since the Moran game. Moran was still undefeated, and the Warriors wouldn't get another chance at them until the last game of the regular season. But if the Warriors beat Hollis Hills tomorrow, they would have played themselves into a second-place tie with Rawson, with a month still to go before the play-offs.

Even with the hard feelings that Gus and Cassie knew still existed between them, the Warriors were coming together as a team, and the two of them knew enough not to let anything get in the way of that. So it was pretty much the same in basketball as it was in school. If you didn't know how much things had changed between them—and in their friendship— you wouldn't have been able to tell by watching them lately, both at practice and in games.

But they knew. Jack and Teddy knew. Without Gus and Cassie talking about it, it was as if they'd made a silent pact to keep the jam-up between them from being a jam-up for a team that was going good.

The silent part wasn't much of a challenge.

NINETEEN

By now, and without Coach Keith making any sort of announcement, Cassie and Brian McAuley were sharing the job of point guard.

Coach kept starting Brian. Teddy, who kept track of the minutes everybody was playing along with everything else, told Gus and Jack right before the start of the Hollis Hills game that over the past three games, Cassie had gotten even more playing time than Brian.

"She's earned it," Jack said. He poked Gus and said, "I think even you would admit that."

"Did I say she hadn't?" Gus said.

"Admit it," Jack said. "She's doing better than you thought she would."

"When did you become her agent?" Gus said.

"Hey," Teddy said, "I'm the one running the numbers. I should be her agent."

"Would it be okay if we just went ahead and played the game now?" Gus said.

"Thought you'd never ask," Jack said.

Hollis Hills was in first place in the league, with just one loss so far, to Norris. And even though none of them had seen the Huskies play in person, they all knew this was going to be Cassie's biggest test so far. It was because of the Huskies' point guard, Fabian Morrell, who'd moved to Hollis Hills over the summer from New York City.

He wasn't all that much taller than Cassie; they all saw that when the Huskies showed up in the gym at Walton Middle. He didn't even look as if he weighed much more than Cassie, Fabian was that skinny. Teddy said he wasn't much wider than one of the cornrows in his hair. He wore high-top, old-school Jordan sneakers, in red and black, which were the Huskies' colors, and as soon as the Huskies started warming up, as soon as the Warriors saw him with a ball in his hands, they understood why he didn't go by Fabian.

He'd shortened it.

He was just Fab.

Like he'd even made a cool move with his name.

There had been a story about him in the Hollis Hills newspaper, one Teddy had found online, that said the coach at Hollis Hills High wanted to put him on the varsity team, even though he was only in eighth grade, but that there was a rule in their district that you couldn't play for a school that you weren't attending.

"They make the rules," Fab said in the story. "I just make plays."

Gus had to admit, that sounded like a pretty fab response to him. When the Warriors were getting ready to huddle up around Coach before the start of the game, Teddy pointed at Fab Morrell with his score book.

"I've been watching him," Teddy said. "I'm thinking I should just give him this book and let him fill in his stats himself."

Teddy hadn't seen Cassie standing behind Jack.

"You're saying that you don't think I can cover him?" she said, giving him the Look.

"Nothing personal, CB3," Teddy said to her. "But I'm not sure CP3 could cover him."

They both knew he was referring to Chris Paul.

"We'll see," Cassie said.

They all saw.

Fab was that good. He dominated Brian in the first four minutes of the game, faking him out so badly with one crossover move that Brian actually fell down. Coach had no choice but to finally call time-out with the Warriors already down by ten points, and try Cassie on Fab. If that didn't work, Gus figured, they'd eventually have to try the same box-and-one on him that they'd used on Chris Charles in the Rawson game.

Over the rest of the quarter, Cassie looked even worse against Fab than Brian had. She was fast, everybody on their team knew that by now. She just wasn't as fast as Fab Morrell, or as quick, because in basketball those could be two separate things. Even dribbling the ball, Fab could beat everybody up the court. Now the Warriors had run both of their point guards at him, and it was a mismatch against both of them.

For the first seven games of the season Cassie had been able to hold her own against the point guards she'd seen. She just hadn't seen anybody like Fab Morrell. None of them had. By Gus's count, he'd either scored or assisted on every Huskies basket in the first quarter. The Warriors were down 16–4.

In the huddle after the quarter, Coach Keith said, "Before I go to one of our tricked-up defenses—well, our *only* tricked-up defense—I want you to take a shot at the playground legend, Jack. You go to point for a little bit. Gus, you move over and play the two, and Jake can play small forward to start the quarter. And Steve? I want you to be quicker getting into the lane when he makes a move to the basket, and use your length on him. We need to make him feel as if he's going up against all of us and not just one of us."

He looked around.

"We good?"

"No."

It was Cassie. Usually Coach did the talking in the huddle, unless he was asking a question. Cassie had apparently decided that this question required an answer. From her.

"Coach," she said, "I can cover that guy."

Gus couldn't decide whether she was speaking out of anger, or frustration, or embarrassment about the way Fab had made her look so far. But he knew her well enough to know how much she hated looking bad, in anything. Fab was making her look bad, and she was taking it personally. It was as almost as if the scoreboard read VISITORS 16, CASSIE BENNETT 4.

Coach turned and looked at her. "And you'll get a chance to prove that before the game is over," he said in a soft voice. "But right now I want to try something different to see if we can get back in this sucker before halftime."

He paused then and said, "Okay?"

Gus knew it wasn't really another question.

"Okay," she said, and then looked away.

Cassie Bennett, Gus knew, didn't lose many stare-downs. She hardly ever backed down. But she did now, just went and sat as far away from Coach Keith as she could and watched as Jack went to point guard and brought the Warriors back. It wasn't as much what he was doing on offense. The Warriors were running the same stuff they had when Brian and Cassie had been in there; they were just making more shots now. No. It was at the other end, where Gus watched as Jack totally accepted the challenge of manning up on Fab Morrell.

From the time Gus and Jack had started playing ball together, Gus had seen how much pride Jack took in his defense. It was the same in basketball as it was in baseball, whether Jack was pitching or playing shortstop. He got as fired up making a good play in the field as he did hitting a ball over the fence, or putting another line drive in play.

While Brian and Cassie had been backing off Fab, giving him too much room because they were afraid he'd drive right past them, Jack started picking him up in the backcourt, getting right up on him, so close sometimes that Gus started to wonder if you could have slipped a ruler in between them. And it threw Fab off his game. As fast as he was, as fast as he kept trying to play, suddenly there was this guy in front of him, slowing the game down.

Jack made one steal right off Fab's dribble. Another time Jack and Gus double-teamed him, and Gus came away with the ball. He drove the length of the court and scored. He made a couple of jumpers off feeds from Jack after that. Jack and Steve even worked a couple of high pick-and-rolls to perfection, and Steve got easy buckets. Right before the half, Jack got out on a break, saw how little time was left, pulled up, and made a three-pointer.

And the game was tied.

As they walked back to the huddle, Gus said to Jack, "We havin' any fun yet?"

Jack turned his head. "Are you *insane*?" he said. "Covering that guy is a *grind*."

"Well, keep grinding, dog."

"All I want to do now is get a drink and sit down," Jack said.

"You want to take a nappie, too?" Gus said.

"That guy makes you play your best every second you're out there."

"You're making him do the same," Gus said. "We got this now."

"Go tell that to Fab," Jack said.

Because Jack had played the whole second quarter, Coach

gave him a rest to start the third, and put Brian back in at point. He left Gus at shooting guard and went with his three bigs up front: Steve, Len Ritchie, Max Conte.

But Fab went back to playing the way he'd played to start the game. In the first minute of the quarter—in *one minute*—he made a steal and a layup, made a three-pointer after a Gus miss, then drove to the basket again, made the shot, got fouled, and made the free throw. Just like that, the Huskies' lead was back to eight points.

Coach called time and put Jack back in, but not at point guard. He put Cassie back in with him. Before they broke the huddle, Coach said to her, "You can cover this guy, right?"

"Right," she said, holding his gaze this time.

He smiled. "Well then, go cover him."

Gus had seen Cassie bring the Look to games she was playing plenty of times before. He had seen it when she really wanted or needed a strikeout in softball, or a goal in soccer. He just could never remember her looking as fierce as she did right now, as she focused on finding a way to stop Fab Morrell.

She had to know she couldn't do it herself; even Jack hadn't been able to do that. Fab really was that good, and a lot better at basketball than she was. Not because he was a boy and she was a girl. He was just better at basketball than everybody in the gym.

But Cassie wasn't going to let him continue to show her up,

just because of the force of his talent. Gus knew how she was wired: this was her chance to prove herself all over again, prove she belonged in a boys' game. Because if she could hold her own against Fab, she could hold her own against anybody.

And Gus felt himself rooting harder for her than he had all season. He had never rooted against her, not for one minute. He just wanted her to make her stand, right here and right now, and not just because it would give their team a better chance to win. Whatever he and Cassie had been going through—whatever they *still* had to go through—you had to respect pride like this.

From the middle of the third quarter until there were two minutes left in the game, Coach Keith left Cassie out there. And she held her own. Fab was still making plays, and shots. He blocked one of Cassie's shots and stole the ball from her once. It wasn't as if she were playing him even. Nobody expected her to do that. But she was close enough, and the game stayed close because of that, and because Gus got hot again, hotter than before, as hot as he'd been all season. It didn't matter who was passing him the ball. Just pass him the ball.

With a minute and a half left, he hit another long jumper. The game was tied at 50. Fab came back, worked a give-and-go with his center, and looked like he was about to make a layup. But Cassie reached in at the last second and got a piece of the ball. He missed. Steve got the rebound and kicked it out to Cassie, who

MIKE LUPICA

started a fast break. On the other side of the court, Gus broke free of his man and into the clear. Cassie didn't hesitate. She stopped and threw a long pass like she was a quarterback in football.

But she threw the ball too far out in front of him, leading him by too much. The ball sailed past Gus and out of bounds. Cassie leaned over and for a moment looked to be in so much pain that Gus thought she might have hurt herself throwing the ball. But she was just mad at herself.

"Stupid!" she yelled.

Gus came running back to her. "You were trying to make a play."

"A stupid play."

"Forget it," he said. "Just get another stop. We got this."

For one brief moment, things felt the way they used to. He had her back. He knew she had his.

Fab ran some clock at the other end. Cassie stayed with him. He started to drive the lane, then pulled up, Cassie as close as she could be to him without fouling, playing him perfectly. He fired up an off-balance shot anyway and got lucky, the ball banging off the backboard even though there was no way he was trying to do that, rattling the rim as it went in. Game tied.

Gus got a great look at the other end, but just as he was releasing his jumper, he saw Jack break free under the basket. Somehow the shot became a pass. Jack caught the ball, shot, made it. Warriors back up by two, twenty seconds left, Huskies with a chance to tie. The Huskies coach called time.

In the huddle, Coach Keith said, "I just want to change up one thing on defense."

Cassie was so far into the game now, so far into her matchup with Fab, that she couldn't help herself. "Please don't take me off him now!" she said. "I can do this!"

She didn't sound as if she were talking about this game, or this play. She sounded as if she was talking about the whole season, all of it.

"Wasn't going to, CB," Coach said. "I was just going to tell Steve to come up and pressure the inbounds pass, no matter who's throwing the ball in. If it's not the center, Len can pick him up."

"Thank you," Cassie said.

"Thank me after we win the game," Coach said. "And one other thing? No fouls."

Jack's guy took the ball from the ref at half court. Steve came up to guard him. Jack dropped back to cover Steve's man, a linebacker from the Hollis Hills football team named Jay Pisante. Cassie stayed with Fab, who broke free of her and took the inbounds pass.

He made his move with ten seconds left.

They had cleared out the left side for him. So it was Fab against

Cassie one last time. Gus was the closest Warriors defender to them. Fab took one last look at the clock above the basket and tried to freeze Cassie with the same crossover move that had put Brian McAuley on the ground what felt like hours ago.

Cassie was still with him.

Five seconds.

If Fab was shooting, he had to shoot now.

Fab gave her one last head fake, lowered his shoulder, and tried to get around her on a right-hand dribble.

Cassie was still with him.

So he stopped and squared up for his jumper, knowing that he was out of time.

And as he did, here came Gus Morales from Fab's right.

Jack would say later that watching Fab and watching the clock at the same time, the shot would have counted. Only Fab Morrell never got it off. Gus knew he was taking a chance by going for the block, risking a foul. But even though Coach had told them no fouls, he always told them something else: *never think about the play you could have made on the ride home.*

He timed his swing at the ball perfectly, almost like it was a pitch he was sitting on in baseball, and knocked it all the way off the court.

He knew it wasn't a foul. Fab knew. The refs saw it was a clean hit. By the time the ball reached the first row of the bleachers, the horn had sounded.

Now the Warriors had won six in a row.

Fab stood and stared at the ball rolling along the front of the bleachers, as if he couldn't believe his eyes. He stared at the ball the way Gus had stared at his air ball at the end of the Warriors' game against the Rawson Raptors. He came over to Gus, nodded, put out his fist so Gus could bump, said, "You got me good," and walked away.

Gus and Cassie were standing at the free-throw line, facing each other.

"We were a pretty good team right there," he said.

"You finally figured that out," she said.

Then she was the one putting out her fist.

"Fab," she said.

TWENTY

They all agreed that being president of your grade at Walton Middle School gave you about the same influence you got from being captain of one of your sports teams.

"It's a beauty contest," Cassie said. "Just between a boy and a girl in this case."

"Well then, Marianna's going to win, isn't she?" Teddy Madden said.

"You're only going to vote for her because you like her," Cassie said.

Teddy wheeled on Gus. "Did you tell—?" He stopped himself. "You don't know what you're talking about."

"I *always* know what I'm talking about," she said. "Or I don't talk."

Jack said, "I know I probably shouldn't be asking this, Cass. But other than when you're sleeping, when *don't* you talk?"

Her response was to punch him in the arm. "You're better than that," she said to Jack.

"Not really."

They were in the third row of folding chairs in the gym, getting ready for the first official debate between Steve Kerrigan and Marianna Ruiz. And while they all knew there really wasn't a whole lot to debate when you were running for this particular office, they were curious to see how hard the candidates would go at each other.

Angela Morales was seated next to her brother.

"Steve thinks the way his father thinks," she said. "He's just never gotten to think that way in public. I want to see if he'll actually do it today."

"He's got some Hispanic friends in school," Gus said.

Angela snorted. "Name three," she said.

"He'll get back to you on that," Teddy said, leaning across Gus.

"The only difference is that Steve doesn't see people like us as a threat, the way his father the mayor does," Angela said.

"Just that we're not worthy of breathing the same air as he does."

Angela had gone from being a volunteer in Mr. Ruiz's campaign to being campaign manager for his daughter, helping her write some of her opening comments today, and her campaign slogan:

Ruiz for president.
Of all of us.

Gus had agreed to help his sister, under the condition that she would do most of the work.

"I will be the brains of the operation," she had said to Gus. "You can be what they call in politics my 'man on the ground.'"

"What will that mean, exactly?"

"You help me make posters and then tell everybody in our grade to vote for Marianna."

"I can handle that."

Angela had smiled and said, "Marianna and I both agreed that you could." And when his sister had asked what he thought Steve's reaction would be to him helping Marianna with her campaign, Gus had told her the truth.

"Bad, I hope."

Now one of the eighth-grade history teachers, Ms. Ciccone, was stepping to the microphone and introducing the three eighth graders who would ask the questions today. She added that this was the first of two debates, to be held over the next two weeks, before there would be one last assembly before the election, when Steve and Marianna would basically give their closing arguments.

Steve was at a podium on one side of the stage. Marianna was at one on the other. Ms. Ciccone said that they had flipped a coin, and that Steve would make a brief opening comment, and then Marianna.

Clearly enjoying himself—the center of the basketball team always loved it when he was the center of attention—Steve leaned down to the microphone and said, "Greetings, fellow eighth graders."

Then he turned to Marianna and said what Brian McAuley had told Gus he was going to say.

"And to you, Marianna: *¿Cómo está?*"

At which point Marianna Ruiz smiled at him and said, "Why, Steve. I didn't know you had a *second* second language."

He bit, as Gus hoped he would.

"What's my other one?"

"Well," Marianna said, looking out at the whole eighth grade, smiling brilliantly as she did. "I think we all know it's English."

It got a huge laugh. It was as if she'd won the debate already.

Teddy leaned over and whispered to Gus, "Was that Angela's idea?"

Gus shook his head.

"No," he said. "That was mine."

"¿Cómo está?" Angela Morales said to her brother. "Really?"

"Maybe his dad is advising him," Gus said.

"Then how the heck did the dad ever get elected?"

They had decided to skip the bus today and take the long walk home. Neither of them had basketball practice, and the day was unusually warm for the middle of winter. So they were walking it.

"The guy's a knucklehead," Gus said. "His dad is one too. They probably come from a long line of knuckleheads."

"Maybe all the way back to the *Mayflower*," Angela said. "Their ancestors were probably happy on that boat: everybody looked like them."

"Marianna crushed him in the debate," Gus said.

"She did," his sister said, "not that I'm sure it's going to matter in the end."

"Why?"

"Because whether he's an idiot or not, he might just win because he's Steve Kerrigan, the mayor's son."

"But did you watch him up on that stage? It wasn't just that

Marianna's last name is Ruiz. The guy acted as if he didn't think a girl was worthy to be running against him, even if he didn't come right out and say it."

"Next thing you know, a girl will think she can be president of the United States," Angela said. She gave him quick poke in the ribs. "Or play for the Walton Warriors."

"You know they're not the same thing."

"A woman running for president or Cassie playing for the Warriors?"

"Cassie."

"Are you sure they're not the same, brother?"

"Hey," he said. "Whose side are you on?"

"Didn't you tell me that you asked Jack the same question?"

"I did."

"And do you remember what his answer was?"

"You know what it was. He said he was on everybody's side."

"So am I."

"So you're on Cassie's side and your brother's side at the same time?"

She nodded. "I am!"

"You're the smart one," he said. "Explain to me how that works."

"I want you both to win in basketball," she said. "But I also want there to be the same chances for girls that there are

MIKE LUPICA

for boys. It's why I hated the way Steve acted today, starting with when he thought he was being clever using a Spanish expression."

Gus said, "It was like he was looking down on her, and not just because he's a lot taller."

"He thinks he's such a star, because of his dad and because of basketball," Angela said. "It was like when Donald Trump ran for president. He thought people should vote for him because he was famous. He talked about making America great again, but every time I saw him give a speech, it was about how great *he* was."

"You followed that a lot closer than I did."

"Mom and Dad say they're trying to raise concerned citizens, remember?"

"You're concerned enough for both of us," Gus said. "And everybody in our family." He grinned at her. "And about half the families in Walton."

"Hey," she said. "You're acting concerned by helping out Marianna."

"You know what I wish her campaign slogan really was?" Gus said. "'Anybody but Steve.'"

Angela laughed suddenly. "My favorite part today was when he got asked about any changes he might make in the Honor Council."

"And he said that he thought we should have only honorable

kids on it," Gus said. "Then he turned to the crowd like he'd said something brilliant and they should applaud."

They walked a few blocks in silence, neither one of them in any hurry to get home, just enjoying each other's company. There were so many things Gus loved about his sister. One was that she wasn't constantly checking her phone the way her girlfriends did.

The other was that she wasn't afraid of silences like this.

But finally she said, "I've got a question."

"Don't make it as hard for me as the debate questions were for Steve."

"What if it had been me?" Angela Morales said to her twin.

"What if it had been you what?"

"What if it had been me who tried out for the Warriors? What if I was as good at basketball as Cassie is? What if it had been me who'd been good enough to play with the boys?"

"You wouldn't have wanted your teammates to be as chafed at you as they are at Cassie."

"What if I didn't care, though?"

"But you would have cared," Gus said, "because you're you and not her."

"You're looking for a way not to answer the question," she said. "I want to know if you would have resented me the way you do Cassie."

Gus knew from experience that his sister could get him

turned around as well as Cassie ever could when they started having a conversation like this. It never got as heated as it used to with Cassie. He hardly ever got angry with Angela. But he knew how persuasive she could be. If she wasn't his sister, he might even have called her pushy.

"It wouldn't have bothered me as much, but it would have bothered me," Gus said. "There, are you happy?"

She ignored the question. "All because I'm a girl."

"No."

"Yes."

"You're putting words in my mouth."

"No," she said.

"Yes, no, yes, no," Gus said. "You're confusing me."

"Not so hard sometimes."

"Nice," he said. "From my own sister."

They were almost home.

"I'm just trying to make you see something," Angela said. "You've got to have a better reason than just thinking Cassie doesn't belong because she's a girl and you're a boy. Because if that's all you've got, you're no different than Steve."

"That is the meanest thing you've ever said to me."

"I've been thinking about it all day," she said. "And you know part of our deal with each other. We can never be afraid to tell each other the truth."

"Wait," he said. "You're saying that you think I'm . . . prejudiced against Cassie?"

He stopped. So did she. They were facing each other at the corner of Spencer, a block before their street.

"I'm just telling you that maybe you and Steve are more alike than you think."

Then she gave him a shove and sprinted away from him, saying she'd race him home.

"I don't want to race you!" he yelled after her.

"Loser!"

Gus just watched her go, thinking about how their mom was always joking that this was about the age that boys figured out that girls were a little smarter and cooler, fell a couple of steps behind them, and then spent the rest of their lives trying to catch up.

Gus saw his sister take a left and disappear like a streak, and felt in that moment as if he'd never catch up, with this girl or any girl.

They had both agreed that Steve Kerrigan was a loser, and not just at the debate today.

Now my own sister is comparing me to him, Gus thought.

So what kind of loser does that make me?

MIKE LUPICA

TWENTY-ONE

Every so often, if you were lucky, you could get one of the courts at the Walton YMCA to yourself.

When Gus and Jack had first started playing rec league ball at the Y when they were in the third grade, back when a final score could be something like 12–10, they used to be at the Y a lot.

On Saturday mornings there would be two games going on at once in each of the Y's two gyms. It was supposed to be their first organized basketball, except when Gus thought back on those Saturday mornings they didn't feel organized at all. It felt like they were playing *dis*organized ball. But what he mostly remembered was what big fun it was when they were little, back when you could barely remember *what* the final score was by the time you got home.

But once a basketball season started now, Gus hardly got over to the Y. In the spring and summer and even in the fall, when the weather was still nice, if he and Jack and Teddy and Cassie wanted to play pickup ball—and they couldn't score their way into the gym at Walton Middle—they would play in the driveway at one of their houses. If it was a bigger game, they'd go play at one of the parks downtown.

Gus wasn't looking for a pickup game on the Sunday after their latest win, against Norris, a rematch with Scotty Hanley and friends that they'd won by fifteen points. He just wanted to shoot around today, work on his game a little bit, see if he could start to feel more consistent outside the three-point line. And with the temperature in Walton down to ten degrees, none of that was going to happen in his driveway.

They had kept their family membership at the Y, mostly because his dad liked to use the weights in the exercise room and swim laps in the Y's Olympic-size pool. So his dad drove them both over when they got home from church.

When Gus walked into the first gym, he saw that there were

a couple of half-court games going on. But the gym next door was wide open.

Hoops heaven.

He went to work, warming up with layups, using both hands, driving from the right and then from the left. After that he shot free throws, like he was getting reps in. Before he left the line, he did something that always helped him get a feel for the ball, and his touch, and his release: he shot the ball with his eyes closed.

He went through the same routine that he'd use when he was shooting free throws in a game, bouncing the ball three times, cradling it in both hands, taking a deep breath. Right before he released the ball, he'd shut his eyes. Not all the shots fell. But Gus wouldn't leave the line until he could make at least five out of ten. Sometimes he wouldn't even look until he heard the sweet sound of the ball hitting the net clean.

Practice with purpose was one of Coach Keith's big things. Gus did that now. He shot left-handed jumpers off the dribble. Sometimes he would bounce the ball hard off the floor, high, then catch and shoot, as if he'd just come off a Jack Callahan screen.

He worked left to right around the perimeter, then back the other way. Finally his shot felt good enough that he went behind the three-point line and started firing away. From the time the season started, he'd been dreaming about a moment when the Warriors would be down two points at the end of a game and he'd make a three to save them.

That was what he kept envisioning in the empty gym, the sound of the ball coming off the old floor loud even when it came off one of the dead spots:

Down two, need a three.

He made one from the left corner. Then he made another one from the opposite corner. Then another from the top of the key. He missed from the left wing, then again, and made himself stay there until he made one.

Gus knew he wouldn't get three chances in a big game. He'd only get one if it ever came down to that for him and the Warriors. And if he ever got to take a shot like that, he was going to make the most of it.

He looked up at the clock on the wall behind the basket and saw that he still had half an hour to go before his dad would be done with his workout. Gus smiled, pretended the second hand was counting down the end of a game, and drained a three from the left corner.

From behind him he heard, "Gustavo, from downtown!"

He turned around, already knowing whose voice it was, and saw Steve Kerrigan standing just inside the double doors, smiling his phony smile, a ball of his own on his right hip.

"How about a game of one-on-one?" he said.

Gus said sure, knowing he had no choice. The best he could do while Steve was warming up was tell him that he didn't have a *whole* lot of time, that he was waiting on his dad.

"No worries," Steve said. "Game of ten, win by two."

He looked at Gus and smiled again, and made Gus think of an expression their mom loved to use: *phony as a two-dollar bill.* Angela had given up reminding her that there actually had been two-dollar bills once. Mom just liked the way it sounded.

Gus just thought she could say that something was phonier than Steve Kerrigan and be more accurate. It usually happened when there was some kind of audience around. But today it was just Gus, an audience of one, watching Steve act as if he were happy to see Gus.

"How cool is this? Two teammates, one-on-one."

"Cool," Gus said.

"We ought to get after each other like this more often, right?"

Yeah, right, Gus thought. *Like we don't get after each other enough already.*

They'd agreed to use Gus's ball. He tossed it to Steve now and said, "Shoot for it."

It turned out that there was nothing cool about the game, or even fun. They weren't teammates getting after each other. They were opponents. And it was like the announcers said on television: these two opponents didn't like each other.

Steve had the size advantage, clearly. Gus was quicker, though not by a lot. He was also the better shooter from the outside, also not by a lot, because Steve could step back and knock down shots himself, with what Gus had to admit was a great-looking release.

It was after they'd each scored twice that Steve staggered Gus with a foul that was way too aggressive for a pickup game on a Sunday morning at the Y.

Gus had gotten past him with a neat head fake and thought he was in the clear for a layup before Steve grabbed him from behind and—or so Gus thought—tried to throw him to the ground rather than give up an easy basket.

"Hey," Gus said.

He didn't go down, but nearly did.

"Got carried away, I guess," he said, but didn't apologize.

"You *guess*?"

Steve shrugged and put his smile back on. "Hey, this is a contact sport sometimes," he said.

Instead of checking the ball to Gus by handing it to him, he threw it now, a lot harder than he needed to. Still smiling. "Not like some class election, am I right?"

So that was what this was about. Maybe Steve couldn't believe his luck when he'd found Gus in the gym. Maybe he'd been waiting for it to be him against Gus like this, no coach around, no teammates, just the two of them.

One-on-one.

"It's just basketball, dude," Gus said.

Steve was already in his defensive crouch, though Gus was thinking maybe he was the one doing that, playing defense even though he had the ball.

"You're right," Steve said. "Just two guys hooping it up."

Gus drove to his right this time, because he was getting more and more confident dribbling with his off hand. Sometimes as he was stopping and rising up to shoot, Steve was able to jab a hand in his chest. Gus made the shot anyway, and didn't call anything, not wanting to give him the satisfaction.

A few baskets later Gus stepped back for a three and Steve ran at him, going for the block with the long reach of his right hand and slapping Gus's shooting hand hard enough that it made him wince and forced him to shoot an air ball.

"Foul," Gus said.

"You gonna call every little ticky-tack thing?" Steve said.

"Wait," Gus said, putting on a fake smile of his own now, "let me see if my left hand is still attached to my left arm."

Steve shook his head, as if disappointed.

"Even Cassie never calls stuff like that when *we* play one-on-one," he said.

Gus shrugged. "She's tougher than me, obviously."

This time Steve handed Gus the ball. "Tell me about it," he said.

They went to 9–all. Gus put down the ball hard on his dribble, got Steve backing up just enough, stepped back, and hit a jumper from just inside the three-point line.

It was game time.

If he scored the next basket, he'd win.

Steve got up close on him when they checked the ball at the top of the key. He wasn't going to concede another jumper, not the way Gus had been shooting the past few minutes. But now Gus used a move he'd been working on, where he rocked back without actually stepping back, then created sudden momentum for himself, a little extra burst, when he moved forward.

The move worked. He was past Steve, driving hard from the left, pushing off his right foot for a layup, but ready for the contact he knew was coming.

Fool me once, he thought.

Steve slapped at Gus's arm, not even trying to make a play on the ball. But two things happened then, almost at exactly the same time: Gus got off his shot with his left hand, which went in. And he came up with his right elbow and caught Steve squarely on the nose.

Direct hit.

They both ended up on the floor. Gus got up first and saw the blood coming from Steve's nose. When Steve took his hand away, he saw the blood too, jumped up, and started for Gus.

"You tried to break my nose!" he screamed.

"Calm down," Gus said. "It was an accident."

"No, it wasn't."

Gus told him he had a towel in his gym bag. Steve told him to keep it.

"I wasn't trying to hurt you," Gus said, "whether you want to believe that or not."

"No," Steve said, "not you, Gustavo. You're everybody's pal. Even the girl running against one of your teammates for class president."

"The election's not that big a deal," Gus said. "And neither is me helping out Marianna."

"It is to me," Steve said.

Then he added this: "I guess you people all stick together, though, right?"

Now Gus was the one taking a step forward.

"You *people*?" he said, stepping on the second word.

If he got any closer to Steve Kerrigan, he could have touched the guy's bloody nose with his own.

"Why don't you explain to me what 'you people' means?" Gus said.

"I think you know," Steve said.

Neither one of them was backing up.

"Yeah," Gus said. "I do know what you mean, the same way I know exactly who you are."

He would never get the chance to find out what would have happened next, where they were going to take this, because now he heard "*Gustavo!*" again.

From his father.

TWENTY-TWO

His father was standing next to the double doors, where Steve had been when he'd called out to Gus, his gym bag in his hand.

But Eduardo Morales never said another word. He just jerked his head to the side to let his son know they were leaving. Now.

Gus turned back to Steve, still not having backed up, eyeballed him for a few more seconds until Steve was the one who broke the stare, and walked away. Gus then walked over to where his basketball had ended up, underneath the basket, collected his gym bag and towel, and left the gym.

He wondered if Steve even knew that Gus's shot had gone in. He also wondered what the call would have been in a game, if Steve would've gotten a whistle for hacking him or if Gus would have drawn an offensive foul because of his elbow.

What he didn't know in his heart was whether he had really been protecting himself, because of the rough way Steve had played, or if throwing that elbow was the same as punching Steve Kerrigan in the nose.

It was something else he would never know, the way he really wouldn't know what would have happened if his father hadn't shown up when he did.

Neither Gus nor his dad spoke until they were in the car.

"Did you hear what he said?" Gus said.

"I heard," Eduardo Morales said, "the way I have been hearing my whole life." He sighed. "But when I was your age, they said even worse. I was a beaner, or a greaser, or a spic."

Gus winced hearing the words, even though his dad had spoken of these things before.

"I'm surprised that Steve didn't say worse," Gus said. "I know those things are in his heart."

That got a chuckle out of his dad. "If you can find it," he said. "When his father said he was speaking from the heart during the campaign, I sometimes wondered whose."

Just being with his dad, feeling his calm, started to make Gus feel more calm and make his anger go away, almost as if he'd left it behind in the gym.

His dad said, "Who won, by the way?"

"I did," Gus said.

"Does that make you feel better?"

"Not much."

His dad turned on the radio, and they listened to music for a couple of blocks, until Gus said, "I might have hit him if you hadn't shown up."

"It looked like you had done that already."

"I mean with my fists."

His father reached over and turned down the music. Then he shook his head.

"No, son," he said. "No, you would not have done that."

"How can you know that?"

"Because if you had fought him, you would have made that boy what he so desperately wants to be, but will never be."

"What's that?"

"Better than you, Gustavo."

His full name had never sounded better.

TWENTY-THREE

Steve Kerrigan ended up with a slight black eye because of the shot he'd taken to his nose. And because he *was* Steve Kerrigan, and could do no wrong—at least in his own eyes, black or otherwise—he told everybody that Gus had lost his temper because he was about to lose the game, and *had* thrown the elbow at him on purpose.

Cassie said that when she'd asked Steve if he really believed that Gus would do something like that, Steve said, "You know the way he acts around me. You think I don't know the stuff he says about me? What do you think?"

Then he piled another lie on top of the others, and said that when he'd just mentioned to Gus that he didn't think it was very cool for him to basically be working on another team—and against a teammate—in the election, Gus had said, "What are you going to do about it?"

"He said I said that?" Gus said to Cassie when they were waiting for their bus.

She nodded.

"And you believe him? Tell me you don't believe him. You know me better than that."

"I know he's the one with the black eye," Cassie said. "And he's the one you do call an idiot or a jerk every chance you get."

For some reason, the buses were late today. It gave Gus a chance to tell her exactly what had happened, how he hadn't even wanted to play the stupid game of one-on-one, and how when it was over, Steve had said what he'd said about Gus and Marianna and "you people."

"If he said that, then that's just plain wrong," she said.

"If?"

"I wasn't there," she said.

"That's exactly what he said. 'You people all stick together.'"

"That would make me want to hit him with an elbow. Or worse."

Gus sighed, loudly. It just came out of him. "I didn't intentionally hit him."

"What do you want me to say?" she said. "It's his word against yours."

"You know me!" Gus said, trying to keep his voice down. "You know that I don't lie, and I don't go picking fights with people."

"I don't want to get in the middle of this. You're both my teammates."

"But you're *my* friend," Gus said. "Have you ever seen me try to hurt anybody?"

"There's all sorts of ways to hurt people."

"I can't believe I'm hearing this."

Their bus pulled up, and the door opened, and the kids in front of them in the line started to get in. Jack wasn't with them today; he was doing some extra work with his chemistry teacher. Neither was Angela. She and Marianna were working on some new campaign posters.

Cassie, looking straight ahead, said, "I can't believe a lot of stuff that *I've* heard from you this season."

When she climbed up the steps, she walked all the way to the back of the bus. Gus sat down in the second row. All he could

MIKE LUPICA

think about on the way home was that Steve had won this time. If Cassie wasn't definitely giving him the benefit of the doubt, she clearly had her doubts about which one of them was telling the truth.

In that way, Steve had already gotten even with Gus.

Steve thought Gus looked bad, at least to him, by helping Marianna. Now Steve had gone out of his way to try to make Gus look bad with Cassie, though Gus seemed to be doing a pretty good job of that by himself lately.

Despite everything that had happened between them, and was still happening, Gus had always just assumed that he and Cassie would work their way through it. Now he was starting to wonder. She kept talking about how much Gus had hurt her. But had it occurred to her how much she was hurting him by taking Steve Kerrigan's side, in anything?

The guy *was* a jerk. And if you lined up with somebody like that, what did that make you? Angela had told Gus that maybe he was more like Steve than he wanted to admit.

But what about Cassie?

He hated himself for thinking about her that way. But there it was, anyway.

Anybody who knew Steve Kerrigan knew that he was as good at knowing when to shut up as he was at being modest. So he wouldn't stop talking about his black eye when they got back to practice, even though you could barely see that he still had one.

"I'm glad Gustavo's on my team," Steve said when they were getting ready to scrimmage. "If he gets my other eye, I'll look like a raccoon."

Gus said, "It might be an improvement," then added, "Just kidding."

"You're about as funny as an elbow to the face," Steve said.

Coach Keith blew his whistle, something he rarely did, and said, "Okay, Mr. Kerrigan. Let it go."

But Steve didn't want to. He kept making comments that only Gus could hear once the scrimmage started. He ignored Gus a couple of times when he was wide open, but Gus was used to that even in the best of times between them. One time Steve cut to the outside instead of toward the basket the way he was supposed to on their "Carolina" play, and Gus's pass to him went sailing out of bounds.

Finally, with about a minute left on the clock, he waited until Gus wasn't looking and threw a bullet pass that hit him in the back of the head.

Gus wheeled around, not believing what had just happened, and was about to say something, but didn't get the chance.

Jack beat him to it.

"Cut the crap," he said to Steve.

It got everybody's attention. Nobody had ever heard Jack speak to a teammate that way.

"Cut what?" Steve said. "It's not my fault he wasn't looking."

"The only way he could have been looking was if he had eyes in the back of his head."

It had suddenly gotten very quiet in the gym. Gus was waiting for Coach to say something. But he didn't, at least for now. Maybe he knew that if Jack was this mad at a teammate, he should get out of his way.

"You've been on Gus all night," Jack said. "Get off him now."

"I don't know what you're talking about," Steve said.

"Yeah, you do," Jack said. "We don't need any of this stuff around this team. Stop bringing it into the gym with you."

"Or what?" Steve said. "You and your boy won't like me? You *already* don't like me."

Now Coach Keith stepped in. He motioned for Gus and Jack and Steve to meet him at half court.

"It's been awhile since I was in the eighth grade," he said, speaking only loudly enough for them to hear. "And what I remember is that I didn't always like my teammates and they didn't all like me. That's just life, is what it is. But what I *also* remember is that I never let it affect the way I played the game. And it's not going to affect the way you guys play the game. Or the next time, I'm the one who's going to get mad."

He grinned then. "And trust me. Nobody wants that."

But even then, Steve didn't know when to shut up. He waited until they were all leaving, then made sure he was behind Gus as they headed for the door and whispered, "Who's going to fight your battle next time?"

Gus didn't turn around, or even break stride. He knew Jack was waiting for him in his mom's car. Mrs. Callahan was Gus's ride home tonight.

"*Yo,*" he said.

From behind him he heard Steve Kerrigan say, "What the heck does that mean?"

"It means me," Gus said.

TWENTY-FOUR

Somehow the Warriors kept winning.

Teddy loved to read about sports history, any kind of sports history. He said he wasn't one of those guys who thought sports started when he got interested in them. He said that there had been a lot of teams that had won championships even though not all the players liked one another, and that he didn't see any reason why the Warriors couldn't do the same.

"You think Derek Jeter and Alex Rodriguez liked each other

when they played with the Yankees?" Teddy said. "No way Jeter liked that guy. But they still won a World Series together."

It was two weeks after Gus and Steve had had their big blowup at the Y and then at practice, the night Jack had called Steve out in front of the team. But the Warriors won their game that week, and this morning had beaten Brenham in Brenham's gym, by six points.

The biggest basket came with a minute left, and stretched the Warriors' lead to eight at the time. Jack missed; Steve got the offensive rebound and threw the ball out to Gus, without hesitation. Then it was Gus who didn't hesitate, whipping a pass right back inside to Steve, who turned and made the baby hook that put the game away.

So at least on the court they were figuring it out, whether they liked each other or not. Cassie had played her best floor game of the season against Brenham. Teddy credited her with nine assists.

Gus and Jack and Teddy were in Gus's room, deciding whether to ask Gus's dad to drive them into town for pizza. Gus had actually invited Cassie to come over too, but she was shopping at the mall with her mom.

While they tried to make up their minds, something they all knew could take some time, Teddy had continued his lesson in Sports History 101.

"Look at the NBA," he said. "I read up on Kobe when he was retiring last year and found out how jealous he and Shaq were of each other when they were winning a bunch of championships with the Lakers."

"They were still taking shots at each other after Shaq retired," Jack said. "And I don't mean jump shots."

"I get it, okay?" Gus said. "You don't have to be good with everybody to play good with them."

But Teddy wasn't done.

"And how about the hated Jets?" he said. He hated on them because he was a Giants fan. "Ryan Fitzpatrick wouldn't even have gotten his starting job that one year if one of their teammates hadn't punched Geno Smith, who was supposed to be the starter, and broke his jaw."

"I get it!" Gus said. "Please stop now."

"I give and give," Teddy said. "And this is the thanks I *get*."

There were two games left in the regular season. The Warriors were still in second place, tied with Rawson and Norris. Amir El-Amin and the Moran Mustangs were still in first, and still undefeated. But as long as the Warriors were undefeated the rest of the way, they were a lock to get one of the four spots in the league play-offs. And they all agreed that the way they were playing now, they would take their chances with anybody, the Mustangs included, once they got to the play-offs.

"I love the way we play Amir to end the regular season," Jack said. "I'd love to give them their first loss."

"And give them something to think about before the tournament begins," Gus said.

He was stretched out on his bed. Jack was sitting cross-legged at the end of it. Teddy was in the chair at Gus's desk, checking his Facebook page.

"We gotta make a call on lunch," Jack said. "I'm hungry now."

"Me too," Teddy said.

"Pizza for sure?" Gus said. They both nodded at him, so he hopped off his bed and called down to his dad and asked if he would take them to town. They all heard him say, no problem, he just needed ten minutes.

Gus launched himself back on his bed and said, "You know what the only bad part of this season is? That it's not more fun." He was staring at the ceiling. "You know what I mean? I should be having more fun."

"You mean because of your beefs with Steve and Cassie?" Jack said.

"Yes," Gus said. "And yes."

"But things seem to be better with both of them," Teddy said. "Especially Cassie."

"They're not. They're just pretty much the same."

"Winning helps things, though, right?" Jack said.

Gus said, "But it doesn't *fix* things."

The room fell silent for a moment. The only sound was the *tap-tap-tap* of Teddy's fingers on the keys of Gus's laptop.

Then Jack said, "You know, there's one thing you haven't tried yet."

"Begging for mercy?" Gus said.

"Close," Jack said. "You could tell her that you were wrong."

Gus sat up, so he was facing Jack.

"But if I tell her that, it would have to be because I thought I *was* wrong," he said.

Jack tilted his head to the side, raised his eyebrows at Gus, and smiled.

"Wait a second," Gus said. "You're saying *you* think I was wrong?"

He turned and looked at Teddy. "And what about you?"

"Don't put me in the middle of this," Teddy said. "I'm just seeing who were the likes on that picture I posted at the end of the Brenham game."

"You mean a like from Marianna?" Gus said.

"Like changing the subject much?" Teddy said.

Gus turned his attention back to Jack, who said, "What's wrong is what's happened between you and Cassie."

"So everything she's done is right?" Gus said. "I know she always thinks she's right. But now you do too?"

Jack put out his hands, like he was a coach in baseball giving a runner the stop sign.

"From the start," he said, "the only one on the team bothered about her being on the team was you. You know that's the truth, right?"

"Your point being?"

"My point being," Jack said, "is that the way she's played has proved her point."

"I never said she wasn't good enough."

"But she thinks that's what you *thought*," Jack said. "And that you thought her being on our team was going to mess us up. But it only did for a couple of games that we might have lost anyway!"

Gus thought back to what Angela had said about him being prejudiced because Cassie was a girl. And about how he might be jealous of her.

"You're saying that I can fix this?" Gus said to Jack.

"May I say something," Teddy said, "without my friend Gus Morales biting my head off?"

"I'll need to hear what you want to say first."

"You're the one who can fix this thing because you're the one who made it a thing in the first place!"

Gus looked at Jack, then Teddy, then back at Jack. "So you two have figured everything out, huh?"

Jack said, "Maybe you need to be what you've been all along with Steve. The bigger guy."

Gus didn't get the chance to respond, because his dad picked that moment to call upstairs and tell them he was ready to roll.

Teddy closed Gus's laptop and popped up from the chair, clapping his hands.

"Technically," he said, "it's time for you to be the bigger girl."

Gus nearly got him with the pillow he threw, but Teddy was already out the door.

TWENTY-FIVE

Their second-to-last game of the regular season was against the Clements Spartans, whom they'd beaten in overtime in their first meeting of the season, in the Clements gym, the only overtime game the Warriors had played.

The Spartans had four losses this season. The Warriors and Rawson and Norris still had two. The way the standings were, this was the same as an elimination game for the Spartans. If they lost today, there was no way they could make it into the top four teams in the league.

After they'd finished warming up, Gus and Jack and Cassie had been talking about the various play-off possibilities, and which teams might face off in the semis, until Jack raised a hand. Gus was actually surprised it took him as long as it did, knowing the way Jack looked at sports.

"You guys are better than me at math," he said. "I don't even *like* math. But here's what happens when I crunch the numbers: If we beat the Spartans, we're 1–0 today."

Cassie grinned. "I tell people all the time, Callahan," she said. "You're like half a genius."

"You want the best reason why we need to be 1–0 today?" Gus said. "Because we could knock our friend at the other end of the court out of the play-offs."

He was referring to Clements's best player, and the guy he would be guarding today. The kid's name was Owen Harris, and they all agreed he was the most obnoxious player in their league. Teddy had even said that if he had to choose between Owen and Steve Kerrigan, he'd take Steve every day of the week.

Owen talked constantly, raised his own hands along with the refs every time he made a three-pointer, and barked out orders to his teammates as if he were the one coaching their team. On top of all that, Gus thought he was a dirty player, looking to get away with a trip or a shove or an elbow to the ribs every time he thought the refs were looking somewhere else. But if you even breathed on him, he whined to the refs. Even his voice was obnoxious.

"I swear after the last time we played them, I heard that voice in my sleep," Gus said.

"You probably woke up screaming," Jack said.

"Like he does every time you get close to him on the court," Cassie said.

And of all the players they'd faced this season, sometimes twice, Owen Harris was the one who'd had the most to say about the Warriors having a girl on the team.

"I'd quit first," he'd said to Gus during the last game, while Cassie was shooting free throws.

"If you feel that strongly about it," Gus had said, "I can't believe you even allow yourself to play against a girl."

"Just hanging around to see if she cries when we beat you guys," Owen said.

Owen had gotten his points in that game, even making the basket that sent the game into overtime, but he couldn't do anything to stop the Warriors from pulling away at the end.

In the handshake line, Gus couldn't resist leaning close to Owen and saying, "Boo. Hoo."

Owen made his first four shots today. Two came with Gus guarding him, one came on a breakaway. The fourth came with Cassie guarding him on a switch. Owen backed her in, then finally turned and shot over her. As he ran back up the court, he waited until Gus looked at him. Then Owen wet his index finger and dabbed it under both his eyes, like he was putting teardrops there.

Gus just shook his head.

Just before the quarter ended, the Spartans' center fouled Cassie on a drive. As she stepped to the line, Owen leaned over and said something to her before he took his rebounding position.

Cassie was still glaring at him when the ref handed her the ball. She knocked down both free throws. When Gus and Jack were walking off the court with Cassie after the quarter ended, Jack asked her what Owen had said.

She waved her hand in front of her as if swatting away a bug.

"He just called me a stupid name," she said. "I don't want to talk about it."

"*What* name?" Jack said.

"A name that stupid boys call girls," Cassie said.

Then she told him what it was. The sound of it coming out of her mouth somehow made it sound even worse than it already was.

"Wow," Gus said.

"Seriously?" Jack said.

"Seriously."

Jack asked if she was okay. She gave him the Look, then gave the same one to Gus.

"This is *so* on now," she said. "Is that okay enough for you guys?"

She walked to the end of the bench and grabbed her water bottle. In a quiet voice Jack said to Gus, "He doesn't get away with talking to her that way."

"Nobody should."

Gus reached down behind the bench for his own water bottle. As he did, he thought of the bad names his dad said people used to call him when he was a boy.

He thought, *Maybe Cassie doesn't think I'm the same friend I used to be.*

And maybe he hadn't been.

But today he was.

Gus hated bullies. Owen might not have been one away from the court, but he was trying to be a basketball bully with Cassie, Gus was sure of it, talking to her when he got the chance—and when he was sure the refs couldn't hear him. Making a show out of blocking one of her shots into the stands. Fouling her a little too hard the one time he sent her to the line.

Gus wasn't going to act like her protector; he'd already found out what it was like when she thought he was fighting her battles for her. The only way to fight back was to get up on Owen and shut him down.

The only points Owen had scored in the second half so far had come on free throws, the last two right at the end of the quarter, Owen getting loose near the basket and putting up a short jumper. Gus came from behind and tried to block the shot, but Owen altered it at the last second, and Gus got him on the arm. Owen, who was a flopper in addition to everything else, ended up on the floor.

"Flagrant!" he yelled.

The ref shook his head. Gus put down his hand, and Owen had no choice but to take it. But as Gus pulled him to his feet, he leaned close and said, "Dude, you sounded kind of like a baby there."

Owen made a few shots in the fourth quarter; he was too good for Gus to shut him out completely from the floor. But Steve Kerrigan was matching him basket for basket. The more he scored, the more either Brian or Cassie fed him. About halfway through the quarter, Brian, who'd been getting into foul trouble a lot the second half of the season, fouled out. It would be Cassie's show the rest of the way. With a little over a minute left, the Spartans' point guard got loose for a layup. But Jack came back with a jumper. The game was tied.

Owen missed. Jack got the rebound and threw a long outlet pass to Cassie. Owen had gotten back on defense, and with none of his teammates back with him, he picked up Cassie. Gus was afraid that she might try to make a move on him and get to the basket, show him up that way. But she was too smart for that. She pulled the ball back out and waited for her teammates to set up on offense.

With six seconds left on the shot clock, Gus tried to set a screen for Cassie, as Jack was doing for Steve near the basket. The play was designed for Cassie to get into the lane and get the ball to Steve.

But as she tried to get around Owen, he stuck his hip out and his leg out and tripped her.

Cassie went sprawling, her right ankle rolling underneath her as she did. She cried out and grabbed the ankle in pain.

The outside ref, his view of the play obscured by Gus, signaled for a block on Owen, as if he'd only seen Owen stick his hip out. But Gus had seen the play clearly and knew that what Owen had done, he'd done on purpose.

Now Owen was the one walking over and reaching down to Cassie with his right hand.

Gus stepped between them as Coach Keith was already kneeling next to her.

"Don't," was all Gus said.

Owen looked at him and knew he meant it, and walked away. Gus never took his eyes off him. He heard Jack say, "We good here?"

"We're good," Gus said.

He wasn't going to say anything more to the guy, despite the punk move he'd just made. He wasn't going to risk getting a technical foul, or even getting tossed from the game by starting something.

Jack got close to Gus's ear and said, "We get him back by getting the game."

"And knocking his butt out of the play-offs," Gus said.

Cassie told Coach she could play. She wouldn't even let him help her to her feet. She tested the ankle by running about halfway down the court. Then she sprinted back to the line.

She missed the first free throw but made the second; Warriors by a point, thirty seconds left. It meant that if the Spartans scored, they won.

But Gus wasn't going to let them score. He wasn't going to let *Owen* score, knowing he'd take the last shot—it was who he was, the way he was wired.

Their coach didn't call time-out. Owen took the ball after Cassie's made free throw and threw it in to their point guard, a slick, wiry kid named Tayshawn Purdy. Gus picked up Owen as soon as he stepped inbounds and shadowed him all the way up the court, as if he were the one bringing up the ball. Tayshawn threw him the ball on the Spartans' side of half court with ten seconds left. Owen crossed over on Gus and got a half step on him, headed for the lane. He pulled up and went up for his shot, with five seconds left on the clock. Gus was in front of him now and went up with him, arms straight up in the air, no part of him touching Owen Harris.

He thought of something Coach Keith always said:

No matter how good a shot looked, when it was contested, it got worse.

Owen shot the ball too hard over Gus, and it banged off the back of the rim. As it did, like a delayed reaction—even though Steve had already grabbed the rebound—Owen tried to flop again, as if Gus had just sacked him the way linebackers sack quarterbacks.

Then he looked at the ref, who actually laughed.

"Um, I don't think so, son," the ref said, and then signaled that the game was over.

Gus wanted to tell Owen Harris that begging for a foul that

way meant he was acting like the name he'd called Cassie. But he had a feeling Owen already knew.

When Gus turned around to go celebrate with his teammates, he saw Cassie staring at him. Then she nodded. He nodded back.

Maybe not the friends they used to be.

But teammates.

TWENTY-SIX

Gus had made up his mind on the way to town. Or maybe Jack and Teddy had already made it up for him. It wouldn't have been the first time that happened, his friends figuring something out before he did.

But he was going to tell Cassie that he'd been wrong.

It might not make things right with her. But it was the right thing to do.

If he'd known things were going to turn out this way between them, he would never have said anything in the first place. He could have kept his objections to her being on the Warriors—or his prejudices, according to his own sister—to himself. It just hadn't been worth the trouble, or the damage it had done to their friendship.

He didn't tell Jack and Teddy that he was going to do it. But he was, the first chance he got. He wasn't going to do it by e-mail, or text, or with a phone call. He would step up and do it in person.

It was his mom who had told him once that sometimes admitting you'd been weak was a way of showing how strong you really were.

"You've been pretty quiet," Jack said when they were paying the check for their pizza.

"Thinking," Gus said.

"That must have been hard," Teddy said.

"Why?"

Teddy grinned. Gus had walked right into it. "Being that out of shape at it," he said.

They were all still hungry, even after pizza, so they walked over to Baskin-Robbins for ice cream. It was never too cold, even in the middle of winter, for Gus to pass up Pralines 'n Cream.

Over ice cream, they went back to talking about Owen Harris, and the things he'd said to Cassie, and the way he'd acted in general.

"Flagrant!" Teddy said at one point, doing a pretty solid impression of Owen's annoying voice.

"He was right," Gus said, "just not the way he meant. Because that guy is a flagrant you-know-what."

"Watch it," Jack said, "or you'll really sound like him."

"I hope I haven't been acting like him toward Cassie," Gus said.

"Not even close," Jack said.

"But you guys would have told me if I did, right?"

Teddy said, "I would've had Jack tell you."

They all laughed. Gus was feeling better already, and he hadn't even talked to Cassie yet.

There was still some time before Gus's dad was supposed to pick them up in front of World Pie, the pizza place. Teddy wanted to look for a book, so they walked up a couple of blocks and stopped at the bookstore.

Then Jack insisted they had to stop at Bob's Sports, because there was a new pair of Air Jordans he just had to see. Even though Gus had gone Under Armour, Jack was still a Nike guy.

They were walking back up Main Street, on their way back to World Pie, when they saw Steve and Cassie coming the other way. Gus felt the air come out of him, as if one or both of them had just punched him in the stomach.

It had been such a good day so far, one that had started with a good win. Then he'd come to a decision, also good, to say what needed to be said to Cassie, once and for all. Only now he felt the same way he had that day when he'd seen Steve and Cassie shooting around in her driveway.

"We just had pizza," Teddy said to Cassie when they were all together on the sidewalk. "But you said you were going shopping with your mom."

"I did," she said. "Technically I still am. She's trying on clothes at True Blue."

It was the best women's clothing store in Walton. Marianna Ruiz's mom was one of the owners.

"I ran into Steve," Cassie continued, "when I went to get a hot chocolate at Starbucks."

"And just like that," Steve said, as pleased with himself as ever, "her day got better."

The way mine just got worse, Gus thought.

To Cassie's credit, she turned to Steve and said, "Yeah. Go with that."

Gus couldn't believe how weird this felt, even though it was four players from the same basketball team—and the team manager—suddenly hanging together on a Saturday afternoon.

Teddy tried to lighten things, as if he were feeling the weirdness too.

"I think the only way her day got better is if hanging with

you is better than watching her mom try on clothes," he said. "But I kind of see it as a jump ball."

"You know, Madden," Steve said, "sometimes you're almost as funny as you think you are."

"Wow," Jack said. "That's a lot of funny. Because he thinks he's more hilarious than *The Simpsons*."

"Don't you mean he *looks* as funny as one of the Simpsons?" Cassie said.

"Is she quick or what?" Steve said. "That's why I asked her to run my campaign the rest of the way."

Gus laughed. The sound just came out of it, loudly. There was no way for him to stop it.

Steve's eyes narrowed. "I wasn't trying to be funny," he said. "That's Madden's deal."

Before Gus could figure out what to say next, Steve said, "What, it's okay for you to run Marianna's campaign but it's not okay for Cassie to run mine?"

"I'm not running her campaign and you know it," Gus said. "My sister is."

"But you're helping."

"If you could call it that."

They were all silent until Cassie, in a quiet voice, said to Gus, "What *did* you find so funny about Steve asking me to do that?"

Just like that, it was as if they'd chosen up sides, and he and Cassie were on opposing teams.

"You're not going to, right?" Gus said.

"Would that be a problem?" Cassie said. "Or should I say, would that be *another* problem for you?"

"You didn't answer my question."

"You didn't answer mine," Cassie said.

"C'mon, you guys," Jack said. "This isn't worth arguing about."

"Who said we were arguing?" Cassie said.

But she wasn't looking at Jack. She was still looking at Gus.

"Maybe the question I should have asked," she said, "is whether I need to ask your permission to help Steve, the way I was supposed to ask your permission to play on our team."

Gus's head was spinning. He was thinking about all the things he had planned to say to her the next time they were together.

But the best he could do right now was this:

"Do want you want, Cass. You always do."

He looked past her and saw his dad's car up the block, about ten minutes too late.

"I've got to go," he said.

This time Gus was the one walking away from her. He'd gotten the last word, just not the one he'd hoped for today.

TWENTY-SEVEN

I t was Angela who came home from school on Monday and told Gus that Cassie had decided not to work on Steve's campaign.

"Did you ask her why?" Gus said.

"I did. She said she just couldn't do it."

"That was it?"

"Pretty much."

"Why couldn't she tell me that in town?"

"Maybe," Angela said, "she thought she didn't get the chance."

Now it was the morning of the Warriors-Mustangs game, at Walton Middle. Last game of the regular season. Play-offs started in a week. If the Warriors beat Moran today, they locked up the number two seed and would be playing at home next Saturday, most likely against Rawson.

But that wasn't the mission today, or the goal. The goal was to ruin the Mustangs' undefeated season.

Gus's parents were out finishing one of their early-morning power walks. Gus and Angela were having breakfast at the kitchen table. In half an hour Jack's parents would pick up Gus and drive him to the game at Walton Middle.

"May I ask a question?" Angela said.

"If it's about Cassie, the answer is no."

"Just one question, I promise."

Gus put his spoon down. "But see, that's how it starts. You'll ask your one question, but then you'll follow that up by telling me what you wanted to tell me in the first place, whether you asked your question or not. So go ahead."

She smiled. "With the question or what I wanted to tell you?"

"Does it matter?"

"Okay," his sister said. "What I don't get is why what

happened between you and Cassie in town changed your mind about telling her you were wrong."

He'd told his sister all about it when he got home that day: what his plan had been. How it had gone wrong once Steve had opened his big mouth, and then Gus had opened his.

"I already explained that," he said. "When she started acting that way in front of Steve—"

"That shouldn't have mattered."

"Well, it did to me," he said. "When she acted that way, almost like she was showing me up in front of him, I just couldn't go through with it, admit being wrong to somebody who's sure she's always right."

He looked across the table at his sister. "I couldn't give her the satisfaction," he said. "Can you at least understand that?"

"Actually, I can. But what you need to understand is that Cassie hasn't changed this season. She's the same wonderful brat she's always been. What *has* changed here is the way you look at her. And not just because she turned out to be the Mo'ne Davis of Walton town basketball."

"I don't want to argue about this."

"Who says we're arguing?"

"That's what Cassie always says!"

"You're shouting."

"I know!" Gus said. "And before you tell me all over again

that I'm prejudiced, guess what? I *am* prejudiced. Against people who think they're better than everybody else."

He could feel himself breathing hard, as if he'd already started warming up for the game.

"You feel better now?" Angela said.

"Yeah," he said. "Yeah, I do. I needed to say that to somebody. Remember when you told me that I might be more like Steve than I want to admit? Maybe it's Cassie who's more like him than she'd ever admit."

His sister reached across the table and patted his arm, smiling at him again.

"Steve can't possibly know everything," she said. "He's a boy."

TWENTY-EIGHT

Gus and Cassie managed to stay away from each other during warm-ups the way they had all week long in school, even when they were in the same group. It was like another skill they had mastered this season, on the court and off:

Managing to be apart even when they were together.

But that didn't matter today, because they had a game to win, together.

"We're playing the champions of the regular season," Coach

Keith told them in the huddle before the start of the game. "And we're going to have to play like champions ourselves to beat them."

From the start you could see how much this game meant to the Mustangs, and to their fans. A lot of them had made the trip to Walton, and were making enough noise as the Mustangs jumped out to a lead in the first quarter that it occasionally sounded as if the game were being played over in Moran. But then Coach Keith made a lineup change he hadn't made all season, maybe one he'd been saving:

He went small.

He played Brian and Cassie together in the backcourt, put Jack and Gus at the two forward positions, and left Steve in at center. He told them to press every chance they got, even after a made basket, and run, and then run some more. And it worked. By the end of the quarter, the game was tied. Coach stayed with their small lineup in the second quarter, telling them that he loved the speed of the game.

With two minutes left in the half, the score was 30–30. There was a break in the action while the refs checked out a problem with the clock, and Amir came over to Gus, grinning.

"You guys gonna make us chase the whole game?" Amir said.

"You chase us," Gus said. "We chase you, right into your first loss of the season."

POINT GUARD

"Bring it," Amir said.

"Isn't that what we've been doing?" Gus said.

They bumped each other some fist. It had been that kind of game, and it wasn't even half over yet. There hadn't been any chirp from either team. If Steve still had hard feelings toward Amir from the first game, he hadn't let on. Or maybe he'd just decided that the game they were playing was too good for anybody to start acting bad.

At halftime, the game still tied, Coach Keith said he was going to give the five players who'd been on the court for most of the second quarter some rest in the third. He also said he wanted the Warriors to slow things down, at least for the time being.

"We can't play a whole game the way we've been playing," he said. "So let's catch our breath a little bit and then get ready to give them . . . heck in the fourth quarter."

"Coach," Teddy said, "you can use the word you wanted to."

Coach Keith grinned. "I think my meaning was clear."

As they walked back out for the third quarter, Steve Kerrigan spoke to Gus for the first time all day.

"You're doing a good job on Abdul today," he said.

Gus closed his eyes and shook his head. Even when Steve was trying to pay you a compliment, he still couldn't help sounding like a complete idiot.

MIKE LUPICA

"You know that's not his name," Gus said.

Steve patted him on the back.

"Whatever his name is, just keep doing what you're doing," he said, then walked over and leaned down and said something to Cassie.

So he didn't hear Gus say to his back, "Yeah, I'll try really, *really* hard."

The Mustangs were ahead by a point going into the fourth quarter. Gus wasn't sure he'd heard a gym sound as loud all season. Coach stayed with their regular starting lineup until halfway through the quarter, when he decided to go small again.

"Let's see what we've got left and what they've got left," Coach said during a time-out, after he'd made his substitutions.

Steve Kerrigan had played Donnie Falco, the Mustangs' center, even this time. And Gus and Amir had played each other even.

"You guys have the same number of points," Teddy said quietly to Gus as they came out of the huddle.

"Don't care," Gus said. "All I care about is us having one more point than them at the end of this game."

With a minute left, the Warriors had just scored the last five points and built a four-point lead. Amir had missed his last few shots. Jack had just made a three. Gus had made a long two, the refs getting together after it and concluding that

Gus's front foot had been touching the three-point line.

Mustangs' ball.

But our game, Gus thought.

They couldn't knock the Mustangs out of the top seed. But if they could close this game out, they were going to feel like an undefeated team going into the play-offs, since they hadn't lost a game since before Christmas. The Warriors were going to be on the kind of roll Amir and his teammates had been on all season.

One minute away.

Maybe one stop away.

Gus knew they had to get the ball to Amir, even if he'd gone cold over the past couple of minutes. When it was all on the line, you went with your best. He was the biggest reason they had the record they did. He was still their best shot, in all ways.

The Mustangs needed a quick score, then a stop of their own. They ran one of their favorite plays, Amir basically running off one screen after another until he finally found some open space.

Gus stayed with him, fighting through every one of them.

He knew the Mustangs were running precious time off the clock, and that Amir had to put the ball up soon. Donnie Falco set one last screen for him. Gus fought through it. But the Mustangs' point guard knew he couldn't wait any longer and threw Amir the ball.

Gus had his left arm stretched out in front of Amir as he heard Jack Callahan yell, "Ball!" Gus turned his head at the last second and managed to deflect the ball over to Cassie.

She was a streak then, dribbling toward the Mustangs' basket, Amir chasing her. But Cassie was aware enough to pull the ball out instead of trying to drive the basket, running more seconds off the clock as the Mustangs' coach had run almost all the way to half court, yelling at somebody on his team to foul her.

Amir finally did, with fifteen seconds left. It was the Mustangs' seventh foul of the half, putting the Warriors into the one-and-one. Cassie calmly went to the line and knocked down both free throws like a champ. The Warriors were up six.

Game over.

Until it wasn't.

Until Amir missed his last shot of the game, a wild three-pointer. Steve Kerrigan got the rebound. And then showed everybody on both teams that he hadn't forgotten the words he'd exchanged with Amir at the end of their first meeting, the last time the Warriors had lost a game.

As soon as the horn sounded he whipped the ball at Amir, like he was trying to throw the ball right through him, and said, "Now who's not as good as he thinks he is, *Amin*?"

TWENTY-NINE

A lot happened at once.

The two refs came running over to stop Steve from getting any closer to Amir. Amir just stared down at the ball in his hands, because as hard as Steve had thrown it, Amir had managed to catch it. Then he looked at Steve, just shaking his head sadly.

Coach Keith came running from the scorer's table, along with the Mustangs' coach, Donnie Falco's dad.

Nobody on the Warriors made a move toward Steve. Gus and Jack were actually closer to Amir. Gus didn't know what to do or say, so finally he just walked over, took the ball out of Amir's hands, and said, "Sorry."

Steve heard him.

"Don't apologize for me!" Steve shouted at Gus.

Gus turned around.

"Actually," he said, "I was apologizing for *us*."

The ref standing in front of Steve said, "Son, I can't give you a technical foul, because the game is over. But if you say one more word—and I mean one more—other than 'sorry,' I will tell the people running this league that you were the first player I ever ejected after a game was over. And that means that if your team has a play-off game next weekend, you don't get to play in it."

The ref said, "Nod if you understand me."

He had Steve's attention. Steve nodded.

Gus noticed Cassie, about twenty feet from the action, just staring at Steve Kerrigan, arms crossed in front of her.

The next thing anybody on the court heard was this:

"Don't you talk to my son that way."

Mayor Kerrigan had decided to join the fun. He looked like an older, heavier, more red-faced version of Steve. Gus saw that his face sure was red now.

"Sir?" the ref said. "Don't *you* talk to *me*."

"He's my son."

"You've made that clear. But unless you're the boy's coach, we are not having this conversation."

"Do you know who I am?"

The ref shook his head.

"I'm the mayor of this town," Stuart Kerrigan said.

Gus saw the ref smile. They'd had him for other games this season, but always on the road. This was the first game he'd reffed in Walton.

"I'm from Rawson," he said. "And with all due respect, sir? I don't care if you're president of the United States. You are not a part of this."

Mayor Kerrigan, they were all about to discover, was about as good at knowing when to shut up as his son was.

"You keep this up," he said, wagging a finger at the ref, "and I'll have your—"

"What?" the ref said. "Whistle?"

Coach Keith then walked the Kerrigans, father and son, back toward the Warriors' bench. Gus heard him say, "If we make this any worse, it will only hurt our team. And no one wants that."

At last the Kerrigans shut up. Coach sat them both down and began speaking to both of them. When he stopped, Mayor

Kerrigan and Steve stood up and followed Coach Keith back onto the court.

Coach turned to Steve and said, "Go ahead."

Steve stuck out his hand. Amir stared at it, then said, "What's my name?"

Good for you, Gus thought.

"Sorry?" Steve said.

"I said, what's my name?"

"Amir," Steve said.

Amir shook his hand then and walked away, nodding in Gus's direction as he did. Gus nodded back at the same time as Mayor Kerrigan walked over and said to the ref, "I'm sorry I spoke to you the way I did."

He put his hand out. The ref shook it. Stuart Kerrigan started to walk away then. Before he did, the ref touched him on the shoulder. Mayor Kerrigan turned back around.

"Coaches talk to refs in this league," the ref said. "Not parents. Remember that next time. Except that there shouldn't be a next time, should there?"

The look on Mayor Kerrigan's face said he didn't like hearing that very much. But he took it. Gus watched him, amazed. He *was* the mayor of Walton. He was supposed to be the boss of their town. Only Coach Keith had been the boss of him. So had the ref.

It was over now, except for this:

As Steve's father began to lead him out of the gym, Steve said something to him and headed in Cassie's direction. But when she saw him coming, she turned her back and came walking over to where Gus and Jack and Teddy were standing.

"You guys ready to go?" she said.

They told her they were. Teddy said this was about as much excitement as he could handle for one day. Gus and Jack agreed. And then, for the first time all season, the four of them walked out of the gym together.

THIRTY

They walked to Teddy's house from the gym. As they walked across the baseball field at Walton Middle, still covered with snow, Cassie fell in between Teddy and Gus.

"No more talk," she said.

"Wow," Teddy said. "He's not allowed to talk? What would you have done to him if we'd lost?"

Jack was behind them. "She would have taken away his cell phone."

"She can do that?" Teddy said.

"Ha-ha-ha," Cassie said. "You guys are hilarious. But I was talking to Gus."

"Sure," Teddy said. "*You* get to talk."

She punched him in the arm. "Shut up, Teddy."

To Gus she said, "You know what I mean. We've done enough talking."

"I know," Gus said. "But there's one more thing I *have* been wanting to talk to you about."

Cassie said, "Tell me when the season is over."

"You're gonna want to hear it."

"Then I'll still want to hear it when the season is over," she said. Then she did a solid Steve Kerrigan impression as she added, "*Okay, Amin?*"

They all laughed. When they stopped, Gus said, "You sure you don't want to hear what I have to say?"

Cassie said, "I just want to talk about basketball until the season is over."

"Then you'll probably want to hear that I thought that was some heads-up move, pulling the ball back out after your steal."

"You mean your steal," she said.

"Whoever's steal it was, you made the right play."

Cassie smiled. "I know," she said.

"Shocker," Gus said.

"Hey," Cassie said. "I said I wanted to stop talking about you and me. I didn't say I was going to stop *being* me."

"Whew!" Teddy said. "*There's* a relief."

"Nobody would ever want *that*," Jack said.

Maybe it was best, Gus thought, at least for now, keeping his feelings to himself. He'd found out the hard way this season how easily he could open his mouth one moment and then stick his foot in it the next.

So he was going to put this small victory with Cassie in with the bigger victory in the game. For a little while, things felt the way they used to between them. He fell back a couple of steps behind Cassie and Teddy and Jack and watched them make their way across Teddy's backyard, looking and sounding as if they were all talking at once.

Looking like a team again.

He quickened his pace to catch up with them.

It was after practice and after dinner on Wednesday night, still almost three full days until the Warriors-Raptors game, that Gus answered the doorbell and saw Marianna Ruiz standing there.

"Hey," he said. "You here to see Angela? She's up in her room."

"Actually, I came to see both of you," she said.

From the top of the stairs behind them, Angela Morales said,

"I got jammed up with math homework and forgot to tell him you were coming over."

Marianna looked past Gus and up at Angela. "So you haven't told him yet?"

"I haven't *asked* him yet," Angela said. "And it's probably best if we do it when we're all together."

"Do what when we're all together?" Gus said.

Angela came racing down the stairs, then poked her head into the living room to see if it was empty. "We can talk in here," she said. "More privacy."

"Privacy to talk about *what*?" Gus said. "I'm getting a bad feeling all of a sudden."

"Don't worry, brother," Angela said. "What we want to talk to you about is a good thing."

"It sounds like some kind of big secret."

"Big opportunity," Marianna said.

"Huge!" Angela said.

Angela and Marianna took the couch. Gus took the chair on the other side of the coffee table from them.

"You want to ask him or shall I?" Marianna said to Angela.

"*Ask me what?!*" Gus said.

"No need to raise your voice," his sister said.

Gus sighed.

Marianna said, "I would very much like you to give my

nominating speech in the assembly on Friday."

The words were barely out of her mouth when Gus said, "Thanks for asking, but no. No way."

"At least he gave it a lot of thought," Angela said.

"I could think about it from now until Friday and still not change my mind," Gus said.

"Well," his sister said, "you *are* doing it. Totally."

"Totally not."

"Here's why you're going to do it," Angela said. "As much as you like to complain about English, you're a terrific writer. It's your way of speaking from the heart—Mom says that all the time. On top of that, you're one of the most popular kids in our grade, because both boys and girls like you, and trust you."

"You make it sound as if I'm the one who should have run," Gus said.

"You probably would have gotten more votes against that guy than I will," Marianna said.

"You give the speech," Gus said to Angela. "You're smarter than I am. Or at least that's what you've told me our whole lives."

"While that *is* true," Angela said, "I'm her campaign manager, and even though Brian is going to give Steve's speech, I don't think a campaign manager doing that carries as much weight. Plus, it will look great having somebody who's the anti-Steve giving a speech for Marianna."

POINT GUARD

"Right," Gus said. "That way I can make Steve more anti-Gus than he already is, going into the biggest game of the year. What could go wrong with that?"

"That will be his problem," Marianna said.

"Which will create an even bigger problem on our team than there already is between us."

"You don't have to talk about him," Marianna said. "We all know the guy's a loser whether he beats me or not, same as his dad is a loser even though he beat my dad in their election."

"I hate public speaking," Gus said.

"Liar," Angela said. "I see how well you do when you have to read your words in front of the class."

"Okay, I'm a good reader."

"Because you're a good writer!" Angela said. "And that's not just me talking, or Mom. Every English teacher you've ever had has told you that."

"And it doesn't have to be long," Marianna said.

Gus looked at the two of them, leaning forward, totally focused on him. He was being double-teamed and he knew it.

"People like you *sooooo* much better than Steve," Angela said. "If you speak for her in front of the class, it might end up making all the difference in the election."

"This isn't fair," Gus said, "the two of you ganging up on me."

"Seriously, it doesn't have to be nearly as long as an English paper," Marianna said. "But you know Angela's right: this could mean the difference between me winning and losing."

What was *it about girls?* Gus asked himself. He wondered if they'd be talking him into things his whole life.

"All I want to do the rest of the week is focus on the Rawson game!" he said.

"You're shouting again," Angela said

"Because I really don't want to do this!"

Angela ignored him. Not a first.

"You can take time to write a short speech and not lose your focus," she said.

From the front hall Gus suddenly heard his mother call out, "Say yes already, Gustavo. You know it's the right thing to do."

"You've been eavesdropping?" Gus said.

"That is a hurtful comment," his mom said. "While I am not as thin as I once was, the walls of this house still are."

Gus said to the girls, "What if I get up in front of the class and choke my brains out?"

"Sure," Angela said, "the way you're always choking your brains out in baseball and football and basketball."

Then Marianna said, "Do you really want to live in a world where Steve Kerrigan is the president of anything?"

Gus was beaten, and he knew it.

"I'll do it," he said. "Now will both of you please leave me alone?"

Angela high-fived Marianna. "You're gonna love it," his sister said to him.

"And Steve is going to hate me more than he already does."

"I don't think it's hate," Angela said. "I think it's more fear, even though he'd never admit that. He's afraid of anybody who's different. It's actually kind of sad."

Gus stood up. So did the girls. Marianna checked her phone and said that her mom would be picking her up in ten minutes.

"Thank you," she said to Gus.

"Don't thank me yet," he said. "You haven't seen my speech." To his sister he said, "Which you're going to help me write."

Angela smiled at Marianna, then at her brother.

"Just think of it this way," she said to Gus. "I'll be just one more girl giving you an assist this season."

THIRTY-ONE

Gus told Angela before school on Friday that he was more nervous about making his speech than he was about the Rawson game.

"No, you're not, and I'll tell you why," she said.

"Sometimes I think I'm surrounded by know-it-alls," he said.

"I am not a know-it-all, but I know this," Angela said. "You can't be more nervous about your speech, because you know how it comes out."

They had spent a couple of hours putting the finishing touches on it the night before. When they finally decided they had the words exactly right, Angela put Gus to work on his presentation.

Gus read the speech. Then he read it again. Angela would occasionally tell him to stop and emphasize this word or that. And she kept reminding him that when he made the speech for real, he should make as much eye contact with the kids in the audience as possible. It was, she said, the key to making a connection with them, which was a key to good public speaking.

"How do you know this stuff?" he said.

"I know things."

"Do you ever."

By the time he'd given his last practice speech in front of Angela, Gus was confident that he had it memorized and could give it without notes if he had to. Angela said he was going to be surprised how little he would have to look down once he got going.

"And if you start to feel yourself getting nervous," she said on the bus, "I'll be sitting in the second row. Just look at me."

"Aren't you worried that your face might make me laugh?"

"Nobody in the gym will be laughing once you start giving this speech," she said, "starting with you. But by the time you finish it, Steve Kerrigan might be crying."

The eighth-grade assembly was scheduled for last period. Gus arrived with Jack and Teddy. And Cassie. As he checked out the crowd, he said to his friends, "I swear, the size of our class has doubled just since I got to school today."

"That would just mean more votes for Marianna," Teddy said.

"Who you so have a crush on," Cassie said.

"I'm just focused on Gus's speech," Teddy said, and Cassie said, "Yeah, Madden. Go with that."

"Any final words of wisdom?" Gus said to them.

"Yeah," Cassie said. "Don't fire up one of your bricks."

"Thanks for the pep talk," Gus said to her.

"Don't mention it."

But then she bumped him some fist. He knew that meant something. Teddy kept telling Gus that he needed to take baby steps to get back to where he used to be with Cassie, and how that was much better than acting like a great big baby.

When everyone was seated, Ms. Ciccone stepped to the microphone and thanked all her eighth graders for being as enthusiastic as they had been throughout the campaign. She also said that she hoped the candidates and their managers and everyone who'd helped them throughout the process had at least a little appreciation for what the men and women who'd run for president had gone through the year before.

"Who knows," Ms. Ciccone said, "maybe someday Marianna or Steve will be the one running for higher office."

Teddy couldn't help himself; a laugh came out of him. He immediately tried to cover it with a coughing fit.

"Steve Kerrigan for higher office?" he whispered to Gus once he had his breath back. "Not if there's really a higher power."

Gus responded by punching him in the knee.

"Shut it," he whispered back.

Ms. Ciccone then announced that because Marianna had won the coin flip and elected to speak second, Brian McAuley would officially place Steve's name in nomination first.

Gus could never figure out what Brian saw in Steve, or why he'd want to hang around with him as much as he did. But Brian was a good guy. He just wasn't much of a speaker and fumbled through his talk, making it sound as if the best reason to vote for Steve was because Steve's father was mayor.

"In conclusion," Brian finally said, "Steve's dad made Walton great again."

"I must have missed that," Teddy said to Gus.

"And Steve will make sure our class is great," Brian said. "So here's next year's president of the ninth grade, my friend and yours, Steve Kerrigan."

"He's got more than one friend?" Teddy said, and then covered his knee with his hand so Gus couldn't whack it again.

Gus was curious to hear what Steve had to say, thinking this was Steve's last chance to act as if he were taking the election even halfway seriously.

He didn't.

"I'm not going to make the mistake I did at the start of the first debate," he said, "and try to speak in Marianna's native language."

He thought he was being funny. The problem was, he *wasn't* funny. Other than a few nervous laughs, what he mostly heard were groans from the audience.

"So I'm just going to stick with good old plain English, the same as my dad did when he beat Mr. Ruiz in their election," Steve said.

Gus glanced at his sister, who winced as if she was the one who'd just been punched in the knee. Or maybe the gut.

"Listen," Steve said, "you guys all know me. So you know what you're getting with me."

Which is the problem, Gus thought.

"Wrapping this thing up," Steve said, "I basically think you should vote for me for the same reason people voted for my dad: we need to represent the real Walton in the ninth grade the same as your moms and dads did. Thank you."

He actually pumped his fist as he walked off the stage.

Ms. Ciccone came back to the podium and told the eighth

graders in front of her that Gus Morales would now place Marianna Ruiz's name in nomination.

Gus made his way to the end of the second row. Steve had sat down in the last seat in the first row. As Gus walked past him, he heard Steve say, "Figures."

Gus stopped, looked down at him, and smiled before he headed up the stairs to the stage. He could feel his heart banging so hard against the inside of his chest it was like it was trying to get out. But as he adjusted the microphone, he did what his sister had told him to do:

He found her face. And in that moment, he felt a surprising calm come over him, as if he was exactly where he was supposed to be.

Angela mouthed three words:

You got this.

Gus looked down at his notes, the two pages he had spread out in front of him. But then he suddenly reached down and folded them and put him in the pocket of the blue button-down shirt he'd worn for the occasion.

Angela had told him to speak from the heart. Now he did.

"Steve just talked about the real Walton," Gus began. "And I guess I'm going to do the exact same thing."

He looked at Angela again. Teddy was on her left, Cassie was on her right. Gus wished he had some water, but he didn't.

So he just cleared his throat and told himself not to rush: this wasn't basketball, there was no shot clock up here.

"You know what the 'real Walton' is?" Gus said, putting air quotes around "real Walton." "It's a place where all that matters, or should matter, is who you really are, and how you treat people. Not how you look."

He looked at his sister again and saw her nod.

"The real Walton," Gus said, "is a place where it doesn't matter whether you have a last name like mine, or Marianna's, or Danny Li's, or Bazil Kazikis's or Jamir Rashad's. Or like President Barack Obama's. What matters is what kind of student you are, what kind of teammate, what kind of friend. *Especially* what kind of friend."

His voice rose a little bit. He made sure not to shout. Angela had told him not to shout, because then he'd sound like just another politician. But he could feel his confidence rising.

Now Gus looked directly at Cassie Bennett.

"In the real Walton," he said, "if you really want to do something, and believe you have the talent for it, it shouldn't matter what your name is, what the color of your skin is." He paused just briefly and said, "It also shouldn't matter whether you're a boy or a girl. Nobody should be allowed to tell you that you can't, or try to hold you back, whether you're running for class president or trying out for a team."

He paused again.

"In the real Walton," Gus said, really stepping on those last two words now, "you get to be who you are and what you want to be, and the rules should be the same for everybody, no matter how much people might try to divide us because of our differences."

He shot a quick look at Steve Kerrigan, because he couldn't help himself: Gus was talking to him as much as anybody in the gym.

Steve looked away.

"For me," Gus said, "the eighth grader who speaks best for what's real and what really matters, in Walton and in our grade, who represents the very best in our grade the way her family represents the very best in our town, is Marianna Ruiz, who I am proud to nominate to be our next class president."

The force of the applause hit him immediately. Gus started to reach down for his notes before he remembered that he hadn't needed them; they were in his shirt pocket.

When he looked back up, he saw Cassie get up and lead a standing ovation.

MIKE LUPICA

THIRTY-TWO

It happened every season, waking up one morning and being amazed at how quickly it had gone by, how suddenly you were playing just to get yourself one more game.

It wasn't as if a lot hadn't happened. A *whole* lot had happened, with Gus and Cassie, Cassie and Steve, Gus and Steve. The Warriors had played themselves into a ditch with those two early losses, and in a league where so many teams would end up bunched near the top, their season could have been over almost as soon as it had begun.

None of that mattered now. What mattered today was that their season was really over if they couldn't beat the Rawson Raptors. Nobody wanted that.

It was Teddy who put it best. They had decided to eat breakfast at his house: Teddy, and Gus, and Jack. And Cassie. Teddy's mom, a real estate agent, was showing a couple of houses early, because even she didn't want to miss the game. So Teddy's dad had come over to make his world-famous flapjacks.

While he was cooking up the first batch, with two frying pans going at once, Teddy said, "This is one of those days when we get to feel like all the teams we watch."

"He's right," Jack said.

"Don't sound so surprised," Teddy said.

"But you are right," Gus said to Teddy. "Our game feels as big to us as any game anybody's playing in basketball today."

From the stove Teddy's dad said, "I was never any good at basketball, but even I'm jealous of Gus and Jack and Cassie today. If you ever competed in anything, you'd still rather be playing the game than watching it. That feeling never gets old, no matter how old you are."

"Even Assistant Coach Teddy Madden feels that way, right, Coach?" Cassie said.

"Yes," he said. "I've prepared you players as well as I can. Now it's just a question of execution."

David Madden groaned. "Is that how Coach Gilbert and I sounded during football season?"

Teddy and Jack and Gus looked at each other and nodded. Sadly, Dad, the answer is yes," Teddy said.

The pancakes kept coming. Gus usually loved them, but he could barely get one down today. His stomach was already doing flips. He was that amped up for the game, which was scheduled for eleven thirty. So he talked more than he ate. They were all talking about the game, about how they might defend against Chris Charles today, what Cassie had learned playing against the Raptors' point guard, Alex Trueba, in the teams' first meeting. The chatter was nonstop, nervous, excited, all at once.

Finally, at ten fifteen none of them could wait any longer and made the short walk from Teddy's backyard to Walton Middle.

They had all been a part of so many big games over the past year. Now came this one, in a little over an hour.

Teddy's dad was right, Gus thought.

The feeling he had inside him, one he knew they all had inside them, even Teddy—that feeling never got old.

Gus Morales didn't imagine it ever would.

THIRTY-THREE

Gus just wanted the day to be about basketball.

Steve Kerrigan had probably hated his speech, as much as everybody else, including Cassie—*especially* Cassie—seemed to love it. Angela said afterward that Marianna didn't have to say a word once she got up there, that Gus had already won the election for her; there was no way Steve was beating her on Tuesday.

But all Gus had been focused on since he walked down the stairs from the stage was beating Rawson.

The Raptors had switched up their starting lineup since the two teams had played in December. Today Gus would be matched up against Tyus Massey, who'd been the Raptors' shooting guard at the start of the season. It meant Gus would have his work cut out for him. Even though he had the size advantage, Tyus had it all over him when it came to speed, and quickness. In soccer they called him Tyus Messi, after Lionel Messi, the streak of light from Argentina and the Barcelona team who many people thought was the best soccer player in the world.

"I watched when Jack covered him in the first game," Teddy said after warm-ups were over. "Watch out when he shoots in traffic, because he leans in and draws a lot of fouls that way. He got away with it a couple of times against Jack, even though it was Tyus who initiated the contact."

"Thanks, Coach," Gus said.

"Go ahead, mock me."

"No," Gus said. "I was really thanking you. You've noticed stuff like that all season, and it's helped."

Jack said, "As good as Tyus is, he does turn into one of those soccer floppers sometimes. He goes down if you even breathe on him."

But there was no threat of that in the first half, at least not for the Warriors, because they were playing as if they couldn't breathe. After everything they'd been through as a team this season, and despite the rip they'd been on since they had lost their first two games, suddenly it was as if this moment was too big for all of them.

And they were playing small. Not small ball. Just small. They were down sixteen points at halftime, and Gus honestly thought it could have been more than that. Chris Charles was dominating Steve. Coach tried going zone against him and using the same box-and-one they'd used in the first game. Nothing worked. Gus only had one basket. Alex Trueba had owned Brian McAuley, and Cassie didn't do much better against him, even though she did make the matchup more of a fair fight. If Jack didn't have fourteen points at the half, they easily could have been down twenty points or more. As it was, the Raptors led 36–20.

Even with the bad endings they'd had to start the season, the Warriors had never looked this bad across an entire half. Gus watched his teammates walk back to the bench after the horn sounded, studied their body language, and worried that some of them, starting with Steve Kerrigan, thought they'd lost the game already.

"They're just too good," Steve said to Brian McAuley when he got back to the bench.

"If their shots keep falling," Brian said, "we have *no* shot."

Cassie slammed her bottle of Gatorade down and stood up.

"Yeah," she said. "I don't see why we should even play the second half. Apparently, we're not playing Rawson, we're playing *Duke*."

"Hey," Steve said to her. "Take it down a notch. I didn't say I was giving up."

"It sounded like that to me," Cassie said.

For the first time all season, Steve Kerrigan was the one getting the Look from Cassie. Everyone on the team could hear her. So could people sitting in the lower part of the stands behind the Warriors' bench.

Gus thought, *She hasn't spoken up like this to anybody on the team this season.*

Well, except me.

"What are you, the captain of the team suddenly?" Steve said. "Maybe you should worry about the guy you're guarding—or maybe I should say *not* guarding—and worry a little less about me."

"At least I don't hang my head every time my man goes around me," Cassie said.

Coach had been at the water fountain when Cassie had called Steve out. He stepped in now and put a stop to it.

"Listen," Coach Keith said. "We all need to stop hanging our heads, because that's the only way we're going to get back into this thing. Now everybody get a drink and take a deep breath before we get back after it."

When Steve was out of earshot, Gus saw Coach grin and say to Cassie, "Maybe you can light a fire under his butt, because I sure haven't been able to do that."

"I hate to lose," she said, keeping her voice low, but with steam still coming off it. "And they sounded like losers."

Before they went out for the second half, Coach said, "I don't want you to get crazy, and get away from all the good stuff that's gotten us this far. But I need you to get a little mad, in a good way. Because they're not as good as they've looked, and we're not as bad as *we've* looked."

The players were in a circle around him. Coach paused and made a slow turn, so that he could look at every face, one by one.

"This isn't the way the story is going to end," he said. "And it's not going to end today."

He told them Len Ritchie would start the second half at center, which meant Steve was going to sit. And he told Cassie to get in there for Brian.

Gus and Jack and Cassie walked out on the court together. Gus said to them, "You ready for the season to be over?"

Jack and Cassie shook their heads slowly.

"Didn't think so," Gus said.

The story really did begin to change, and the game with it,

two minutes into the second half, the Warriors having already scored the first two baskets of the third quarter.

Chris Charles, guarded by Gus in a switch, missed a short jumper. The long rebound tipped off Tyus's hands, and then Max Conte's, and was on its way out of bounds. Because Max had touched it last, the Raptors were going to retain possession.

Except that here came Cassie Bennett.

Alex Trueba was closest to the ball and probably could have saved it if he had to. But he didn't have to, because it was going to be the Raptors' ball. So it looked as if he were just boxing out, trying to keep the Warriors' players away from it.

He never saw Cassie coming from behind, laying out like she was doing a racing dive, reaching out at the last second with her right hand and not just keeping the ball in play, but somehow directing it over to Gus.

As Gus reached for the ball, he heard Jack call out from behind him.

And Gus knew in that moment, from all the basketball he and Jack had played in their lives, that Jack had read the play and run out, toward the Warriors' basket. Gus didn't hesitate, or look to see exactly where Jack was. He just grabbed the ball and, without looking, threw it as hard as he could over his head, trusting that Jack was somewhere in the area.

He was. The pass was almost too far in front of him. But Jack chased it down at the top of the key, took two dribbles, and laid the ball in.

Cassie to Gus to Jack.

Just like that, the Raptors' lead was down to ten. The home crowd went crazy. The Raptors' coach called time, wanting to stop the Warriors' momentum, maybe sensing that the game really had just changed.

This time the Warriors didn't walk off the court with their heads hanging, the way they had at the end of the first half. They sprinted, like it was a race to see which one of them could get back to the bench first.

Coach said, "I assume you guys practice that play on your own?"

Gus grinned. "Constantly." He turned to Cassie and said, "You okay?"

"Perf."

"I had to take some points off the score on your drive, Cass," he said. "I think your legs were a little bent at the end."

Her response to that was throwing Teddy a high five that tried to take his hand off. "Okay," he said. "That hurt."

By the end of the quarter, the Raptors' lead was down to four, 40–36. At the start of the fourth quarter Steve got a put-back and Jack hit a jumper, and for the first time since 2–2, the game was tied.

It was still tied with six minutes left.

Then four.

Gus had gotten a breather to start the fourth quarter. So had Cassie. Jack had gotten some rest at the end of the third. When Coach called time with three and a half minutes left, he told them he was going with Gus, Jack, Cassie, Steve, and Jake Mozdean the rest of the way.

"We don't have to play mad anymore," Coach Keith said. "Just as hard as we have all year."

Cassie turned to Gus. "Let's show them the real Walton now," she said.

They all agreed later that what happened next wasn't just amazing to be a part of. It had been amazing to just watch. With everything on the line for their team, Gus wanted the ball. So did Jack. So did Cassie.

Just not Steve Kerrigan.

It wasn't as if he disappeared down the stretch. He was actually doing a good job on Chris Charles now, and getting rebounds. He just refused to shoot the ball, even when he had a good look down low. As soon as he caught the ball, he was looking to get rid of it, to Gus or Jack, or Cassie, or Jake. He was either afraid to shoot, or afraid to miss. Or both. The kid who seemed to go through life thinking he was better than everybody else now thought he wasn't good enough to fire up a single shot.

It didn't stop the rest of the Warriors from matching the Raptors basket for basket. With just under two minutes left, the Warriors went ahead by two, their first lead of the game, when Gus hit an open jumper from the left side. Then Jack hit one from the right. But Chris Charles came back and made a tough shot in traffic. Steve fouled him. Chris made the free throw. Steve forced a pass at the other end when he should have shot; Tyus came down and banked home a runner.

The Raptors were ahead by one, forty-seven seconds left.

Coach Keith called his last time-out. In the huddle he told Cassie to forget about running a play. He just looked at Gus and Jack and said, "One of you guys get open, and she'll get it to you."

"Sounds like a plan," Gus said.

"If we're ahead at the end and they have to foul, we make the shots and win," Coach said. "If it's tied at the end and we get the ball with enough time left, we push it, and score, and win that way."

"Even better plan," Jack said.

"Enough with the plans," Cassie said.

Coach tapped the side of his head with his index finger. "All part of a larger plan," he said.

Steve was the first out of the huddle. Gus moved quickly to catch up with him. "Don't pass up another open shot. If it's there, take it. Or just go tell Coach to put Len back in."

Steve looked at Gus and tried to say something. But it was as if he couldn't even speak. So Gus did.

"If I'm covered, I am going to throw you the ball," he said. "And if you don't take the shot, then when this game is over, I'll take a real shot at your nose." Then he quickly added, "Just kidding."

Then he said what the ref had said to Steve that day. "Nod if you understand me."

Steve Kerrigan at least managed that.

When the ball was in play, Jack set a screen for Gus. Gus waited until Jack's feet were set, not giving the ref a chance to call a moving pick. Then he came around, wide open, and didn't hesitate, squaring himself up and putting up a jumper. But Tyus fouled him hard enough from the side that the ball barely left Gus's hands. Two shots. Gus went through his routine, made the first shot, nothing but string. He thought he'd put a perfect release on the second one too, but it was just a couple of inches long, hit the back of the rim, and bounced into Chris Charles's hands.

Thirty-eight seconds left. Game tied.

The Raptors' coach elected not to call time-out. Even if they ran the thirty-five second clock almost all the way down and missed their last shot, there would only be a few seconds for the Warriors to advance the ball.

The Raptors passed the ball around on the outside until there were fifteen seconds left. Jack had switched and was on Chris Charles. He had him completely smothered. Chris threw it over to Tyus.

Gus was on Tyus, who drove into the lane and did what Gus had been waiting for him to do the whole game: he leaned in and tried to create contact and get a whistle.

But Gus was ready for the move. He got a couple of feet in front of Tyus and set his feet, arms straight in the air. He was too far away from Tyus for there to be any contact at all. It was almost as if the air between him and Gus tripped him up, made him stumble and fire up an off-balance shot.

Ten seconds left.

Jack grabbed the rebound, passed the ball to Cassie, went and filled one wing. Gus took the other. Steve was ahead of the pack.

Cassie did what Coach had told her to do: she pushed the ball. Like she was the fastest kid in the game now.

Jack ran across the court and set one last pick for Gus. Gus

244   MIKE LUPICA

was open again. Nobody fouled him this time. But just as he was about to release the ball, Chris Charles came running at him, arms so high Gus couldn't see the basket.

But he could see that Steve Kerrigan was open.

And Gus did exactly what *he'd* said he was going to do.

He passed him the ball with four seconds left.

There was no time for Steve to do anything except shoot, banking the ball off the board and through the basket.

Warriors 58, Raptors 56.

They were in the finals.

When Steve broke away from his teammates, he walked over to where Gus was standing with Teddy Madden.

"Thanks," he said, putting out his hand.

Then he added, "Gus."

THIRTY-FOUR

The eighth graders voted during first period on Tuesday. Ms.
Ciccone told the school before the vote that the results
would be announced before school let out.

At lunch Angela and Marianna joined Gus and Jack and
Cassie and Teddy. Gus asked Marianna if she was nervous. She
said she totally was not.

"This isn't like your championship game in basketball," she
said, "even if some our classmates are treating it that way. This

isn't about finding out who's better, the way you guys are going to find out against Moran on Saturday."

The Moran Mustangs had won their semifinal against Norris. So the Mustangs and Warriors would meet for the third time this season, third and last, this time for the championship.

Marianna said, "The election isn't an election at all for most of the kids. It's a popularity contest, like we're totaling up Facebook likes."

"But you *are* better than Steve," Teddy said.

"I think he could beat me at basketball," Marianna said.

"You know what I mean," he said. "You are the best one to represent our class."

Gus said, "You want to know the best part of this whole thing? I actually think that it might have made Steve a little smarter."

"Just not smarter than Marianna," Angela said. "Or better for class president."

"No," Cassie said. "But Gus is right. He might have become a better guy."

"No doubt," Jack said. "Look at the way he acted with Gus after the Rawson game."

"Yeah," Teddy said, "but that's only because Gus practically forced him to shoot the ball."

"I just threw him the ball," Gus said.

"It was more than that, and you know it," Cassie said.

"I wasn't asking the guy to be my best friend," Gus said. "Just give us our best chance to win."

"Maybe it wasn't the election that made him a better guy," Angela said. "Maybe it was you, brother!"

The bell sounded.

"Basically all I was really telling him was what we've been told our whole lives," Gus said. "If you're afraid to even try, you have no chance."

That got a smile out of Cassie. "Really?" she said, dragging the word out. "I've never heard that one."

Then, for the first time in a long time, maybe the first time all season, she punched him in the arm.

As Gus and Marianna made their way down the hall to their English class, he said, "Be honest: you're not even a little bit nervous?"

"I'm really not," she said. "You know when I really *was* nervous? The night they were counting the votes when my dad ran against Steve's dad. Now *that* was an election that mattered, because my dad really represents the best of our town."

"Well, I'm still going to wish you good luck."

"And I'll thank you for wishing me good luck," she said. "But I'll be fine whatever happens."

It was just the two of them, standing outside the classroom.

"Just for the record?" Gus said. "You *are* better than Steve, at least in all the ways that matter."

Marianna Ruiz smiled at him.

"Thanks," she said.

When Ms. Ciccone's voice came over the PA system, she reminded the eighth graders that she wasn't going to announce the final vote count. So they were never going to know if Marianna or Steve had won by a landslide, or by a single vote.

And in the end, Gus knew, it didn't matter.

What mattered was hearing Ms. Ciccone saying congratulations to their grade's new president, Marianna Ruiz. As soon as she did, a cheer went up not just in history class, but all the way up and down the halls.

Gus didn't see Marianna until they were all waiting to board their buses a few minutes later. She was usually a shy girl, but when she saw Gus, she came running up the sidewalk and gave him a hug.

"You did this," she said, "with that amazing speech you gave."

"Nope," he said. "This was all you."

"How about we agree that it was both of us," Marianna said. "Or all three of us, counting your sister."

Marianna took a step back now and gave Gus a long look,

and in that moment he thought her big eyes looked full.

"The Ruiz family and the Morales family against the world," she said.

"Or just for the real Walton," Gus said.

"Not just the real one," she said. "The best one."

THIRTY-FIVE

The game between the Warriors and the Mustangs was scheduled for one o'clock on Saturday in the new gym at Moran High School that had just opened this season, because the league wanted to do the championship game up right.

"It feels like Super Bowl Sunday," Gus said to his dad on the short ride over to Moran. "Just on Saturday."

"Try not to think of it that way," his dad said. "That year when the Panthers lost to the Broncos in the Super Bowl, I heard one of the commentators say that as good as the Panthers had been that season, for a lot of them who'd never played in a Super Bowl it would be like stepping onto the surface of the moon. Then most of them, even Cam Newton, played that way. When you tell yourself a moment is oh-so-big, sometimes you make it too big and forget it's still just a game."

He gave Gus a quick sideways glance. "Do you understand, Gustavo?"

"I do, Dad."

"Or are you just saying you do?"

It made Gus smile. "I might do that sometimes. Just not today."

His mom would come later with Cassie's mom, and Jack's, and Teddy's. Jack and Cassie and Teddy were being driven to Moran by Jack's dad.

Normally Gus would have been with them. But his dad asked if the ride over could be just the two of them today. Gus said that was fine with him. And having listened to what his dad had said, and absorbed it, he was glad that it was just the two of them.

"You are," his dad said, "exactly where you are supposed to be, and not just with your basketball team."

"Now that I don't understand."

His dad nodded. "What I'm saying is that you find out

MIKE LUPICA

things about yourself across every season you play, and you have found out those things, especially your ability to make big shots in the clutch. But this season, I think you found out important things about yourself as a person, as well."

"You mean I was dumb about Cassie and then got smarter as the season went along," Gus said.

"Not just smarter, about how you look at girls," his dad said. "But I think stronger, too."

"I still don't know much about girls," Gus said.

His dad said, "Think of it as a subject you're trying to master in school."

"I just want to get a passing grade someday."

That made his dad laugh. "Don't we all," he said.

They were in front of Moran High School by then. Gus's dad turned off the car and then pulled Gus across the front seat to him with his strong right arm.

"Go in there," he said to Gus, "and play a game you will remember when you are as old as I am."

"I'll try."

"One last piece of advice," his dad said. *Aprovecha el día.*"

Gus knew what it meant. It was an expression his dad used a lot.

"Seize the moment," Gus said.

Nothing left now but to play the game.

• • •

As good as the first two games between the Warriors and Mustangs had been, this one was even better.

The Warriors led 32–30 at halftime. Whatever nerves Steve Kerrigan had shown at the end of the semifinal against Rawson, he was playing his best all-around game in a while, maybe his best of the season. Cassie wasn't outplaying the Mustangs' point guard, Pat Palmer—no one expected her to do that, even with the way she'd just kept getting better as the season went along. But she was playing him even, and that was enough. And Gus and Jack were knocking down enough open shots.

On defense Gus wasn't shutting down Amir, but he was containing him, and not letting Amir do what he was capable of doing sometimes, which was get so hot you imagined steam coming off his shooting hand.

To Gus, the first half felt like a blur, as if they'd been playing running time. It seemed to have gone by that fast. The only bad thing that had happened to the Warriors—a bad thing and a big thing—was that both Jack and Steve were in foul trouble.

Jack never got into foul trouble. He hadn't come close to fouling out of a game this season. But he picked up his second foul, an offensive foul, with thirty seconds left. Teddy tried to remind Coach Keith that it was Jack's second, but Coach had walked down the bench to shout out defensive

MIKE LUPICA

instructions for the Mustangs' last possession of the half. By the time Teddy got his attention, it was too late for Coach to sub somebody in. And then with one second showing on the clock, and Jack having picked up Amir on a switch, he was called for a shooting foul, even though Gus thought Jack had gotten all ball.

Amir managed to miss both free throws, but the damage had already been done. When the Warriors got to the bench, Coach said to Jack, "That one is on me. I should've gotten you out of there."

Jack, who never blamed anybody for a mistake he'd made in sports, who never pointed a finger at anybody, shook his head.

"Yeah, Coach," he said. "And you definitely shouldn't have even put yourself in position to get a whistle with one second showing on the clock. What sort of idiot would do something like *that*?"

Coach grinned. "So I guess I better not do anything dumb like pick up my fourth if my coach puts me out there in the third quarter."

"Definitely not," Jack said. "That would be beyond dumb."

They all went to get drinks, happy to be able to catch their breath for a few minutes. When the second half was about to start, Coach Keith gathered the players around him and said, "Well, I've got to be honest: I'm not too happy right now."

He had Gus's attention for sure, because he thought they'd played their best in the first half, that the moment hadn't been too big for them.

He waited along with his teammates to hear what Coach would say next.

"What I'm unhappy about," he continued, "is that this is probably the last half of basketball I'm ever going to get to coach you guys." He smiled, turned to Cassie, and said, "And girl."

"Coach," she said, "I'm one of the guys by now, don't you think?"

"Got it," Coach said to her.

He was kneeling in the circle and looked up. "But if this is going to be our last half together, how about we just go out there and crush it? Would that be okay with you guys?"

"*Yes!*" the Warriors yelled.

Then Gus said, "My dad's got this expression he used on me on the way over: *aprovecha el día*."

"What the heck does that mean?" Steve Kerrigan said.

To him, and to the rest of his teammates, Gus said, "It means 'seize the moment.'"

"Works for me," Steve said.

The game stayed close throughout the third quarter, neither team ever leading by more than a basket. But then, right before the third quarter ended, Coach put Jack back in the game, and he committed his fourth foul. Donnie Falco, the Mustangs' center, had beaten Steve cleanly with a neat head fake and reverse pivot, and had a clear path to the basket. Jack moved over to cut him off, and Gus thought Jack had clearly established position before Donnie plowed into him.

But the ref didn't hesitate: he tapped his hips with his hands and called Jack for a block.

A minute later Steve picked up *his* fourth foul. It was on another switch. You had to do a lot of switching with the Mustangs, because of all the screens in their motion offense. This time it appeared that Steve had gotten all ball trying to block an Amir jumper.

Amir got the whistle. Steve's face got red, the way it did right before his head would explode sometimes. Gus was afraid he was going to say something to the ref, or Amir, and maybe get a technical foul.

But then he looked over at Gus, the closest teammate to him. Gus gave a quick shake of his head, pleading with his eyes for Steve not to say or do anything dumb.

And he did not.

He just put his hand up in the air and walked back to the bench as Coach Keith replaced him with Len Ritchie. As he passed Gus, he said, "I got it clean."

"I know."

"At least I kept my mouth shut for once."

"Know that, too."

With Jack and Steve both on the bench, the Mustangs got ahead six early in the fourth quarter, the biggest lead for either team in the game. But Gus hit a three, and then he and Cassie ran a textbook two-on-one break. Cassie threw him a perfect bounce pass; Gus finished with a left-handed layup and got fouled by Pat Palmer. He made the free throw. The game was tied at 54.

It was 59–58, Warriors, when Coach put Jack and Steve back into the game with four minutes left, knowing he couldn't wait any longer.

But Jack fouled out a minute later, trying to go over Donnie's back for a rebound.

Steve fouled out two plays later, a bad reach-in on Amir when he just should have let him make a layup. Amir made both free throws. Moran led, 64–63.

Ninety seconds left.

Coach Keith called his second-to-last time-out.

On the way over to the huddle, Cassie said to Gus, "I guess it's you and me now."

He bumped fists with her.

"You and me," he said.

"About time," she said.

Coach told them not to rush, that it was all right to run

some clock to get the shot they wanted, because the next basket, for either team, was going to feel like even more than that.

"I don't have to tell you that this is probably going to be a last-shot game," he said. "Team with the ball at the end wins."

Just like football, Gus thought. And like a lot of other games they'd played this season. But none of those games had been for the championship.

They inbounded the ball and worked it around on the outside as the shot clock ran down. Gus finally broke loose from Amir. Cassie threw him a hard two-hand chest pass over on the left wing; Gus was a couple of feet inside the three-point line.

He buried the shot.

Warriors by one.

Last minute.

Last-shot game, Gus thought, *in a last-minute season.*

The Mustangs elected not to call their last time-out. Now they were the ones working the ball around on the outside. Finally Pat Palmer faked a pass to Amir, even though everybody in the gym thought the ball had to end up in his hands, and elected to work a give-and-go with Donnie Falco. He threw it to Donnie, Donnie gave him a perfect bounce pass, Pat had the step he needed on Cassie and laid the ball in.

Mustangs, 66–65.

Coach Keith didn't call his last time-out either.

He stood next to where Teddy was sitting at the end of the scorer's table, smiling, and maybe for the last time this season, told them this:

"Play."

Cassie passed the ball to Gus. Gus threw it to Jake, who threw it back to Gus. Who threw it over to Cassie.

Ten seconds left.

Now or never.

"Go!" Coach Keith shouted, over the noise of the crowd.

Gus was in the left corner. Len Ritchie ran over and set a screen, one that put Amir a step behind the play. Gus ran out toward the three-point line, where the most space was. That was where the shot was, the three-pointer he'd dreamed all season about making.

That was where the game was, and their season.

Cassie was about to throw him another two-hand pass. But at the last moment Pat Palmer jumped in front of her. So the only way for her to get Gus the ball was to throw the pass behind her back. The pass he'd seen her working on that day in her driveway with Steve Kerrigan.

The pass was nearly perfect.

Gus caught the ball, turned, squared himself up, saw the clock above the backboard as clearly as he could see the basket.

Three seconds.

He could have taken one dribble, to get closer. They didn't need a three to win, even though the game winner had always been a three in his dreams.

A Steph three.

Gus let the ball go. As soon as he did, he knew. Sometimes you just knew.

It hit nothing but string. Warriors 68, Mustangs 66. Horn. Ball game. Championship.

Belleza, he thought.

A beauty.

THIRTY-SIX

The first thing Cassie said to him:

"Show-off."

"Look who's talking," he said. "Behind-the-back? Really?"

"I've been practicing it."

"I know," he said. "Saw you one day in your driveway with Steve."

"You were spying on me?" She put her hands on her hips, but she was smiling.

"Picking up pointers," he said. "From my point guard."

"It was the only way for me to get you the ball so you could make your hero shot."

"By making a hero pass."

"What else," she said, "did you expect from me?"

They had celebrated his shot with each other, and their teammates, and then gotten into the handshake line. They finally went and sat down on their bench, waiting for the trophy presentation on the court to begin. Gus sat next to Cassie. Jack was on the other side of her. Angela and Marianna had come down the stands to sit behind them. Marianna was next to Teddy, which made him look like the happiest kid in the gym, and he hadn't played a minute.

Gus couldn't help but notice that Steve Kerrigan had moved back a row, to sit next to Angela. Gus heard him saying, "You know, if you'd been *my* campaign manager . . ."

He paused just long enough for Angela to say, "You still would have lost."

They all laughed. Gus wondered, just briefly, if Steve understood that even in the gym at Moran High School, the best Walton was right here.

It was taking longer than anybody expected to do the ceremony, because there was a problem with the microphone. While they tried to fix it, Gus stood up, pulled Cassie up with him, and said, "Come on."

"Where we going?"

"The season's over," he said.

She said, "Oh."

They walked past Steve and Angela and Marianna and Teddy and made their way to the last row of the bleachers and sat down there, backs against the wall.

"Let's get this over with," Cassie said, "so we never have to talk about it again. Okay?"

"Okay," he said.

Then he said, "I was wrong, Cass. I'm sorry. I acted like a jerk."

"Is that it?"

"It's not enough?"

Then she really smiled. "I'm sorry too."

"For what?"

"You weren't the only one acting like a jerk. So was I."

"Not like me."

"Well, of course not!" Cassie Bennett said. "But you weren't totally wrong. At the beginning, it was more about me than it was the team. And nothing should ever be more important than the team."

"Except for friendship," Gus said.

"Except for that."

The sound system was fixed. They both heard the president of the league's board of directors announce that the trophy presentation was finally about to begin.

"As great as my pass was," Cassie said, "your shot was even better, gotta admit."

"My mom's right!" Gus said. "Girls really are brilliant."

Cassie stood up first.

"You know what I really can't wait for?" she said. "Baseball."

And she took off down the bleachers.

"Wait, you mean softball, right?" he called after her. "As in *girls'* softball?"

"For me to know," she called out over her shoulder, "and you to find out."

Then she was taking the bleachers two steps at a time, flying one more time, laughing her head off. And one more time Gus watched her and thought something he'd thought about her before:

Boy, what a girl.

He ran to catch up.